Something passed between them.
Could it be sexual awareness?

Lissa cleared her throat and said, "You should find everything you need."

"Thank you." Sullivan's voice wrapped around her like a plaid tartan on a winter night.

Oh, brother. "Well," she said, trying to ignore the feelings she didn't know how to deal with. "I guess I'll leave and let you get unpacked."

"Don't," he said.

Huh? "Don't what?"

"Don't leave yet." He tossed her a boyish grin. "I spotted a bottle of wine on the kitchen counter. Will you join me for a drink on the front porch?"

The offer took her aback. But it also excited her.

She tried to tell herself it was simply a continuation of business. Yet she couldn't help making a wee bit more out of the invitation than was probably wise for someone with a virgin heart ripe for the picking.

And ready to bruise.

D0733679

Dear Reader,

It's that time of year again—when every woman's thoughts turn to love—and we have all kinds of romantic gifts for you! We begin with the latest from reader favorite Allison Leigh, *Secretly Married,* in which she concludes her popular TURNABOUT miniseries. A woman who was sure she was divorced finds out there's the little matter of her not-so-ex-husband's signing the papers, so off she goes to Turnabout— the island that can turn your life around—to get her divorce. Or does she?

Our gripping MERLYN COUNTY MIDWIVES miniseries continues with Gina Wilkins's *Countdown to Baby.* A woman interested only in baby-making—or so she thinks—may be finding happily-ever-after *and* her little bundle of joy, with the town's most eligible bachelor. LOGAN'S LEGACY, our new Silhouette continuity, is introduced in *The Virgin's Makeover* by Judy Duarte, in which a plain-Jane adoptee is transformed in time to find her inner beauty…and, just possibly, her biological family. Look for the next installment in this series coming next month. Shirley Hailstock's *Love on Call* tells the story of two secretive emergency-room doctors who find temptation—not to mention danger—in each other. In *Down from the Mountain* by Barbara Gale, two disabled people—a woman without sight, and a scarred man—nonetheless find each other a perfect match. And Arlene James continues THE RICHEST GALS IN TEXAS with *Fortune Finds Florist.* A sudden windfall turns complicated when a wealthy small-town florist forms a business relationship—for starters—with a younger man who has more than finance on his mind.

So Happy Valentine's Day, and don't forget to join us next month, for six special romances, all from Silhouette Special Edition.

Sincerely,

Gail Chasan
Senior Editor

Please address questions and book requests to:
Silhouette Reader Service
U.S.: 3010 Walden Ave., P.O. Box 1325, Buffalo, NY 14269
Canadian: P.O. Box 609, Fort Erie, Ont. L2A 5X3

The Virgin's Makeover

JUDY DUARTE

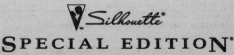

SPECIAL EDITION

Published by Silhouette Books

America's Publisher of Contemporary Romance

Special thanks and acknowledgment are given to Judy Duarte
for her contribution to the LOGAN'S LEGACY series.

To the special ladies who love my youngest son as their own:
Lydia Bustos, a wonderful sister-in-law and *tía* who spends hours at
Chuckie Cheese and pretends to enjoy some of the same movies, over and over.
Sheri Marotte, a talented teacher who became my friend and overlooked more
than a fair share of tardies when my early-morning writing time went into extra
innings. Soledad "Chole" Mendez, a great baby-sitter and friend who provides me
with immeasurable peace of mind whenever my little boy is in her care.
Thank you, ladies, from the bottom of my heart!

SILHOUETTE BOOKS

ISBN 0-373-24593-9

THE VIRGIN'S MAKEOVER

Copyright © 2004 by Harlequin Books S.A.

Visit Silhouette at www.eHarlequin.com

Printed in U.S.A.

Books by Judy Duarte

Silhouette Special Edition

Cowboy Courage #1458
Family Practice #1511
Almost Perfect #1540
Big Sky Baby #1563
The Virgin's Makeover #1593

Silhouette Books

Double Destiny
"Second Chance"

JUDY DUARTE,

an avid reader who enjoys a happy ending, always wanted to write books of her own. One day, she decided to make that dream come true. Five years and six manuscripts later, she sold her first book to Silhouette Special Edition.

Her unpublished stories have won the Emily and the Orange Rose awards, and in 2001, she became a double Golden Heart finalist. Judy credits her success to Romance Writers of America and two wonderful critique partners, Sheri WhiteFeather and Crystal Green, both of whom write for Silhouette.

At times, when a stubborn hero and a headstrong heroine claim her undivided attention, she and her family are thankful for fast food, pizza delivery and video games. When she's not at the keyboard or in a Walter Mitty–type world, she enjoys traveling, spending romantic evenings with her personal hero and playing board games with her kids.

Judy lives in Southern California and loves to hear from her readers. You may write to her at: P.O. Box 498, San Luis Rey, CA 92068-0498. You can also visit her Web site at: www.judyduarte.com.

THE PORTLAND PRESS
Tragic Accident Pulls At The Heartstrings Of City

Portland, OR, 1977—A tragic car accident on Shore Avenue has left one woman dead and her pregnant daughter in a coma, throwing this close-knit community into a tizzy of activity and grief. Witnesses say a truck slammed into the sedan, leaving little question as to who was at fault. "This thing comes barreling down the road, swerving and scaring people half to death!" one man told the *Press,* visibly shaken by what he saw. The victims were identified as Jane Maddison, 34, and her daughter, Olivia Maddison, 16. Both were rushed to Portland General Hospital where Olivia's babies—that's right, triplets—were delivered by emergency C-section and placed in the PICU. Hospital sources tell us that offers to raise the children have been pouring in as news spreads that their mother is fighting for her life and daddy dearest seems to be nowhere in sight. Now their fate lies in the hands of the pediatric staff, with hopes that someone out there will claim responsibility for these tiny victims....

Prologue

Portland, Oregon—1976

"I'm pregnant."

Jared Cambry's gut clenched as he looked at Olivia in disbelief. "But we only did it once. Are you sure?"

The sixteen-year-old blonde glanced down at her worn leather sandals and kicked at a dandelion that grew in the grass at the park where they'd met. She looked up and caught his gaze. "Yeah. I'm sure."

Jared wanted to bolt, wanted to call her a liar. Instead, he blew out a ragged breath. "I don't know what to say."

"I was surprised, too," she said. "I guess neither of us planned on having a baby."

She could say *that* again. He'd just been accepted to Arizona State. And last time his parents had taken him to visit, the football coach had said that he had a good shot at a quarterback position in the fall—maybe even first string.

He looked at the teenage girl who'd just given him the worst piece of news he'd ever heard.

"I know we're young," Olivia said.

Young? Heck, he'd only had his drivers' license for a little over a year. And though old enough to drive, she still rode a bike. They should be thinking about college. And summer vacation. Not a baby.

Besides, it's not as though they'd ever dated. They'd met at a party a couple of months ago, and it had just happened.

Two weeks before the party, he and Megan Phillips, a pretty, redheaded cheerleader he'd gone out with since the fall, had broken up. He was still nursing a broken heart and a wounded pride. And he wasn't in the party spirit—until Olivia had come along, holding two glasses of cheap, fruit-flavored wine.

Olivia had a pretty smile and a way of making him forget about the obnoxious college guy Megan had dumped him for.

Neither of them had been virgins, but the experience had still been awkward. And Jared had a feeling she'd been disappointed.

He'd driven her home afterward, and they'd exchanged phone numbers. But he hadn't called her.

And when she'd asked him to meet her today, he'd been surprised.

"We could maybe date for a while, get to know each other better," she said.

They could date? His mom and dad would come unglued if he brought home a girl from the wrong side of the tracks. They had their hopes set on their only son meeting a debutante, or at least someone whose parents belonged to the country club set.

And even if Jared was willing to go out with Olivia, his family was relocating to Scottsdale about the same time he moved to the dorms at ASU. They said the move was for business purposes, although he suspected they wanted to be near their only child in Phoenix.

"What are you thinking?" she asked, eyes snagging his and demanding some kind of answer.

Heck, he was thinking about all kinds of things. College. Playing football. Maybe taking some pre-law and business courses.

And the sudden realization that his once charmed life was going to hell in a broken-down baby buggy.

Only one solution came to mind. "I'll pay for an abortion."

"What?" Olivia asked, voice raised an octave.

"An abortion. I'll get the money. And I'll drive you there and wait while it's done. That way, your mom won't find out."

"No way. I know having a kid isn't convenient for either one of us. But I'm keeping this baby."

She couldn't be serious. Olivia and her mom lived in a rundown, rusted-out trailer on the outskirts of town. How the heck was she ever going to raise a kid?

And even if he got a part-time job flipping burgers while attending school, he wasn't going to be able to contribute too much. Her keeping the baby was a bad idea—for both of them.

"You've got your whole life in front of you," he said. "Why would you want to tie yourself down?"

"Because babies are a blessing. And God wouldn't have let me get pregnant if there wasn't a good reason for it."

Jared rolled his eyes. He didn't think God had anything to do with the mistake they'd made. And he couldn't see how having a kid at his age would bless his life.

Not now.

Not ever.

Chapter One

Portland, Oregon—2004

"I'm pregnant."

Lissa Cartwright, who'd been slouching in a cushioned patio chair on the deck, nearly dropped her morning cup of coffee and sat up straight. "You're what?"

"Pregnant," her bright-eyed sister said.

"That's great. Congratulations." Lissa managed a smile. She couldn't be happier, yet the excitement had an ambiguous edge.

Last year, her sister had married the love of her life, a man who adored her. And having a baby had always been Eileen's dream.

Lissa's too, she supposed. That's what made the news so bittersweet.

"You look surprised."

No, Lissa wasn't actually bowled over by the announcement, but as usual, when her sister achieved one of those heart-touching milestones, Lissa felt a wee bit envious. "I just didn't expect to hear it so soon. Or so early in the morning."

Eileen laughed. "You didn't think I'd drive all the way out to the vineyard for breakfast, did you?"

"No." Lissa adored her younger sister, but Eileen wasn't a morning person. Not like Lissa.

In fact, the two young women weren't anything alike, but there was a good reason for that. Seven months after Lissa had been adopted as an infant, her mother had given birth to Eileen.

Lissa wasn't sure when she'd begun to feel like an outsider. Maybe on the day her parents sat her down and told her about being special, about being chosen. About her being their very first baby girl.

That's when Lissa began to take a good hard look at the differences between her and her sister.

Eileen was petite and vivacious, a strawberry blond, just like their mother. And Lissa was tall and introspective, with plain brown hair. God only knew who she resembled—certainly not anyone on the Cartwright family tree.

Still Lissa had to give her mom and dad credit for trying to be fair. They were great parents. And they were good to her. She had no complaints.

After all, how could they not love their *real* daughter more?

Besides, Eileen was everything Lissa wasn't. And their differences went beyond appearance—something Lissa had learned in the fall of first grade.

One day after school, their mother had enrolled them in a dance school and bought them new black-patent-leather tap shoes. Mom's enthusiasm had been contagious, and both girls had been ecstatic and ready for their very first lesson.

Before long, Eileen was dancing her little heart out—Shirley Temple style. All the while, Lissa clomped around like a pack mule in army boots.

Fortunately, Ken and Donna Cartwright had done a good job of pretending to be equally proud of both girls. But the tap instructor hadn't been quite as tactful.

But who could blame her? Lissa had seen the proof played out loud and clear on the family home videos of the dance recitals.

Yet that didn't overshadow one important fact. The girls shared a genuine love for each other—and for their parents.

"Have you told Mom and Dad?" Lissa asked.

"Not yet. I will, as soon as they get in from their morning walk."

From her seat on the deck, Lissa scanned the rolling hillsides of Valencia Vineyards, where sturdy vines nourished premium grapes. She loved the fertile land and the bounty it produced. The vineyard was the one place where she actually belonged, where she could thrive and be herself.

That's why she started each day with breakfast on the backyard deck, under the protection of the overhang when it rained and out in the sunshine when it didn't.

She spotted her parents near the new, state-of-the-art winery, walking hand-in-hand, their love for each other impossible to ignore.

Maybe that's what Lissa envied. The sense of truly belonging. Of loving and being loved.

"Look." Lissa pointed toward her parents. "They're coming this way."

"Good. I can't wait to tell them, especially Mom. You know how she is about babies." Eileen rolled her eyes and laughed. "Remember how embarrassed we used to get? I've never known another woman to get so goofy whenever she spotted a little one at the mall or in the grocery store."

"I remember," Lissa said. "And you're right. Mom will be thrilled to have a grandchild."

Especially since Eileen's baby would be a *real* grandchild.

The old insecurities seemed to settle over Lissa, but she adored her sister. "I'm so happy for you. I know how much you love Dan."

Eileen reached across the glass tabletop and squeezed Lissa's hand. "I really hope that you find a special man someday. Someone who appreciates you."

"Thanks," Lissa said, although that wasn't likely. Her shyness made her steer clear of serious relationships.

And at this point, it seemed that life—and love—had passed her by. After all, how many twenty-seven-year-old virgins were still walking the face of the earth? Not many, she would wager.

And since she rarely left the vineyard or winery, Lissa would probably go to her grave never having experienced a night of romance or passion—other than in those books her sister gave to her.

Of course, she didn't admit that to anyone. Not even Eileen.

Instead, Lissa said, "There aren't too many special guys who come around here."

"Well, you need to get out more. You've become a workaholic since I got married."

That was true. Lissa had poured her talents into running the vineyard—from farming to the business end. Deep down, she hoped to prove herself, although she wasn't sure who she wanted to impress. Her parents? The world? The faceless biological parents who'd given her away? Or maybe just herself.

Either way, she'd dedicated her life to the family vineyard and winery. And she was good at what she did. She had a head for business and had soaked in every bit of knowledge her dad shared with her as a vintner.

A muted little bark sounded from the sliding door,

and Lissa spotted her new puppy scratching at the glass, trying to get out.

"Looks like Barney woke up and is raring to go." Lissa glanced at her watch. "I hate to leave you on the deck alone, but I have to go to work."

"Don't you want to be here when I tell Mom and Dad?" Eileen asked.

Lissa gave her sister a kiss on the cheek. "I've got a business meeting in a few minutes, and I've got to look over a few files ahead of time. This is your special moment with Mom and Dad. You can tell me all about it later."

"Who are you meeting?" Eileen asked.

"A business consultant."

"A man?" Her sister sat up straight, nearly knocking over her glass of fresh-squeezed orange juice.

Lissa clicked her tongue. "Don't get your hopes up. His name is Sullivan Grayson. Doesn't that sound a bit old and stodgy? Besides, Dad met him in some tournament at the country club. And you know most of the guys he plays golf with are retired."

"And married," Eileen added. "Okay, so maybe another interesting man will come along for you."

"Yeah. Maybe," Lissa said, not at all convinced. Then she took her dishes into the house, eager to get back to work, to return to the world where she could shine.

Once inside the kitchen, she put the dishes in the sink, while the rascally pup jumped at her feet, trying to get her attention by whining and yapping. When her hands were free, she picked up the little dog.

Barney nuzzled in her arms, then gave her several wet kisses on the cheek.

"I love you, too, little guy." Lissa smiled wistfully.

At the rate things were going in her life, the closest thing to a baby she would ever have was this wet-nosed bundle of joy.

And the closest thing to romance and lovemaking she'd ever experience was waiting for her in one of the paperback novels on the nightstand in her bedroom.

Thirty minutes later, in the wood-paneled vineyard office where Lissa spent most of her time, she heard a car pull up and assumed Sullivan Grayson had arrived. She quickly organized the files she'd spread across her desk, ready to meet the man her father had hired to help the vineyard over a financial slump.

With the assistance of the topnotch consultant and investor, they hoped to create a marketing strategy to promote the new blend of varietals Lissa had developed and jumpstart the struggling, family-owned vineyard.

A light rap sounded at the door.

"Come on in," she called.

As a tall, broad-shouldered man entered, the dark walls seemed to close in on them, and Lissa nearly fell out of her swiveled desk chair.

From the open doorway, the morning sun highlighted a dark shade of burnished-copper in his hair and gave him a rugged, mystical aura that stirred her imagination. His face and stance reminded her of a young Scottish laird.

He wore khaki slacks and a green button-down shirt, open at the collar. No tie. Yet, for a moment, she wondered what he would look like in a kilt, with a broadsword in hand.

"Hello." He flashed a crooked smile. "I'm Sullivan Grayson."

There had to be a mistake. She'd expected an older gentleman who'd been doing business long enough to achieve the mile-long résumé of successful ventures her father had shown her. Not someone whose lively eyes and flirtatious smile made her feel like a gawky adolescent.

A hodgepodge of words seemed to jam in her throat, but she cleared her voice and uttered a belated, "Hello."

"You must be Lissa Cartwright," he said, picking up the conversational ball she'd dropped.

She nodded, then stood and extended an arm across the desk in greeting. "How do you do?"

Gosh, could she get any more stiff and formal than that?

Sullivan gave her hand a gentle squeeze, sending a tingle of warmth to her core.

Her knees wobbled, but she didn't think he'd noticed, and she tried desperately to regroup, to swallow her surprise and ignore the heady attraction to a man who was *way* out of her league.

Still, she couldn't help staring, taking inventory, so to speak. Nor could she help thinking of him as a Scottish highlander standing on a windswept moor— ready to battle a foe of the clan. Or to tease the lassies.

Oh, for Pete's sake. She scolded herself and tried to rein in the silly fantasy provoked by those historical romances her sister had given her. Lissa knew better than to waste her bedtime hours reading that unrealistic fluff, no matter how much she secretly enjoyed them.

She slowly pulled her hand from the Scotsman's grip, aware of the calluses on his palm that belied the image of the manicured businessman she'd expected. ''Won't you have a seat?''

He took the leather chair across from her, then shot her another grin that continued to rock her usually calm nature.

Where in the world was her dad? He'd get this conversation on the right track.

''My father will be coming along shortly,'' she said, reminding herself that this was a business meeting. Nothing more. Nothing less.

Besides, what would a good-looking, successful guy like Sullivan Grayson see in a woman like her?

He scanned the room until his gaze landed on the tri-colored bundle of fur chewing on a red rubber doggie ball by the potbellied stove in the corner. "You have a cute puppy."

"Thanks. His name is Barney."

"I like dogs." Sullivan flashed her another one of those grins that rattled her senses. "And dog-lovers."

She cleared her throat, hoping it would also clear her mind of a fantasy that had become far too vivid. "We can wait for my dad. Or we can get started. Your choice."

"Whatever you're comfortable with."

She wasn't comfortable at all. Not with him or this meeting.

"Your father mentioned you've developed a new wine," he said.

"Actually, it's a new blend of varietals." Lissa clasped her hands on top of the desk, glad to steer the conversation and her thoughts away from the Scottish highlands and back on Valencia Vineyards, where they belonged.

Men like Sullivan Grayson didn't take a second look at women like her. And if he did? Good grief. She wouldn't know which way to run.

Sullivan studied his new client's daughter. Lissa Cartwright was an attractive woman, even though she didn't seem to know it. Or maybe she preferred a plain-Jane image, intentionally downplaying her looks by wearing her hair in a bulky, spinster-type bun and hiding her figure behind baggy gray slacks and a lackluster blouse.

She wasn't a beauty, but he'd still felt a spark of attraction when he'd first spotted her behind that desk. Maybe it was those mesmerizing green eyes that held his attention and made him want to tease a smile from her, just to see them come alive.

He figured she'd felt something for him, too. At least her nervousness suggested she had.

But Lissa Cartwright was definitely off-limits. After all, Sullivan never mixed business with pleasure. And since he was working for her father on a family-owned vineyard, he'd put his interest on permanent hold.

Besides, she had business savvy. And from what he'd learned after researching Valencia Vineyards, she was too serious-minded to be considered dating material, especially for a man who'd learned the hard way to keep his relationships light and meaningless.

Since his divorce at the ripe old age of twenty-five, Sullivan preferred his women to have nothing more going for them than a pretty face, a great body and an impressive rung on the social ladder.

The door opened, and Ken Cartwright entered the office. He extended a hand to Sullivan. ''Forgive me for being late. My daughter, Eileen, just announced she's expecting a baby. And, needless to say, I couldn't disappear until my wife stopped bouncing off the walls.''

Sullivan smiled. ''I take it that she's settled down now.''

"She's still a bit giddy." Ken chuckled. "You have no idea how much my wife loves babies."

"And you don't?" Lissa elbowed him, her lively green eyes taunting her father.

"Okay," Ken said. "I admit it. My wife and I are both suckers for toothless grins."

"I wonder how they'd fare in an old folks' home?" Lissa asked, flashing a smile at Sullivan that sliced right through him.

He couldn't seem to escape her gaze. She had the most amazing eyes he'd ever seen. And when she smiled, her face lit up.

"Shall we get down to business?" Ken asked.

"Yes," Sullivan answered, a bit too quickly. He needed to focus on what he'd been hired to do, and not on a fascinating pair of verdant green eyes that were more than a little distracting.

At lunchtime, Lissa's mother, Donna, and her sister, Eileen, brought a tray of sandwiches and a pitcher of iced tea for them to eat in the office. Eileen kept making goofy, isn't-he-perfect-for-you faces, mouthing things like, *You go, girl* and pointing toward Sullivan when he wasn't looking.

Lissa wanted to clobber her sister. For goodness' sake, it didn't take a brain surgeon to see that the man was a looker. But she also knew he wouldn't be the slightest bit interested in her.

Of course, she'd gotten used to Eileen's efforts to help. In high school, Lissa had become a bookworm and an honor student, but she'd had very few friends. And no dates to speak of, other than Milt Preston, the guy who played Ichabod Crane in the "Legend of Sleepy Hollow" play.

Eileen had talked Milt into asking Lissa to the Christmas formal. As awkward as the experience had been, Lissa had appreciated her sister taking on a matchmaker role back then, but she didn't really appreciate those same efforts now.

When her mother—thank goodness—finally managed to drag Eileen back to the house, Lissa blew out the breath she'd been holding.

For Pete's sake. She was nervous enough. She certainly didn't need a cheering section at a game that was lost before it even began.

Fortunately, her dad and Sullivan had been oblivious to the girl talk, or so Lissa hoped. And the three of them had eaten lunch while talking over business strategy.

By four in the afternoon, the initial meeting finally ended.

Ken was the first to call it a day. "Lissa, I promised your mother I'd help her grill steaks this evening. Will you take Sullivan to the guest house and help him settle in?"

"I'd be glad to." Lissa still felt uneasy around the man. But she'd best get used to it. Sullivan would be staying at the winery until they'd hammered out the details of the new marketing plan. Then his work at

Valencia Vineyards would be finished. And he'd leave without a backward glance.

"You two may as well get to know each other," Ken suggested. "I have some family obligations to take care of, so you'll be spending a lot of time together."

Don't remind me about dealing with the consultant on my own, Lissa wanted to say. Instead, she offered a pleasant grin—the kind she'd practiced over the years when asked to do something she wasn't comfortable doing and would prefer to delegate to someone else.

"My father's favorite uncle fell and broke a hip," Lissa explained to Sullivan. "And there were a few complications, so Dad will be going to San Diego soon, and you'll be working with me."

"Not a problem." Sullivan flashed her another smile that accelerated her pulse.

She called Barney, who'd been chewing on the frayed edge of the throw rug that sat in front of the potbellied stove. When the pup continued to ignore her, she scooped him up, carried him outside and deposited him on the ground, where he immediately began to sniff around until a twig caught his attention.

Sullivan followed behind. "I need to get my bags out of the trunk. Is it a long walk? I can take my car, so it'll be parked near the guest house."

"No, it's just ahead. And you really can't park any closer than this. See the little suspension bridge that leads to the big house?"

"Yes."

She pointed beyond the wooden structure that spanned the fishpond, toward the quaint guest house she'd always thought of as a cottage. "It's just across the lawn."

They stopped long enough for Sullivan to retrieve a suitcase from the trunk of a sporty, silver-gray Mercedes and for her to snap a leash on Barney.

"Lead the way," Sullivan said, with that flirtatious grin that made her heart rate go bonkers.

Was it her imagination? Or did he keep sliding a glance her way?

No way. It had to be her imagination. Maybe he found her an oddity. Or a novelty of some kind. That had to be it, because she never harbored any unrealistic expectations when it came to men.

"It's nice out here," he said, scanning the lush lawns that surrounded the house.

"I can't imagine living anywhere else." And she couldn't. Living on the vineyard, being a part of the land, was one of the best things about being adopted by the Cartwrights. Their love, of course, was another. Even if Lissa didn't quite fit in, she never doubted their affection.

As they reached the wood-planked front porch of the guest house, she turned the antique brass knob and opened the door. "It's not much, but it's cozy."

Actually, Lissa thought the little house was pretty special. She and her mom had decorated it in a country French decor, with café-style window coverings, a blue plaid sofa and a coordinating floral, overstuffed easy chair.

"It gets pretty chilly at night." She pointed to the thermostat on the light-oak-paneled wall. "You can adjust the heat to your comfort."

He nodded toward the stone hearth that boasted a stack of firewood, kindling and matches. "I'd rather have a fire."

So would Lissa, if she were staying in the cottage. A fire was cozier. And more romantic.

Darn it. Those blasted romance books were getting to her again. And the sooner she could box them up and chuck them into a blazing fire, the better off she'd be.

"There's a kitchenette," she said, "in case you prefer to take your meals alone. But knowing my mom, she'll insist that you join us."

"I eat most of my meals in restaurants, so I'll be looking forward to some home cooking."

"Well, good. Mom will be pleased." Lissa would be, too, but she battled the girlish rush of excitement. "I'll show you the rest of the place."

As she entered the hallway and glanced through the open doorway to the bedroom, her gaze landed upon the blue-and-white checkered comforter on the double bed she'd made up yesterday.

She caught a whiff of his musky, highland scent—mountain fresh and wild—and felt his presence close in on her, as though she might find him inches away, if she turned around.

Her pulse and her breathing seemed to escalate, but her feet remained rooted to the spot.

"Nice room," he said.

Unable to help herself, she turned and caught him merely inches away.

Watching her.

And he wasn't smiling—at least, not in a teasing sort of way.

Something passed between them, although she wasn't sure what it was. Could it be sexual awareness?

Nah. Impossible. Not on his part, anyway.

She cleared her throat, which seemed to be another habit she'd mysteriously acquired today. "The bathroom is down the hall, next to the linen closet. The cupboards and shelves are stocked, so you should find everything you need."

"Thank you." His voice wrapped around her like a tartan plaid on a winter night.

Oh, brother. Those books were going right into a moving trash truck the first chance she got.

"Well," she said, trying to ignore the rush of sexual awareness she didn't know how to deal with. "I guess I'll leave and let you get unpacked."

"Don't," he said.

Huh? "Don't what?"

"Don't leave yet." He tossed her a boyish grin. "I spotted a bottle of wine on the kitchen counter."

"It's our sauvignon blanc. I thought you might like to have a glass now and then."

"That sounds good now. Will you join me? On the front porch?"

The offer took her aback. But it also excited her.

She tried desperately to tell herself it was a continuation of business. A way of relaxing over drinks. The kind of things businessmen did all the time.

Yet she couldn't help making just a wee bit more out of the invitation than was probably wise for someone with a virgin heart—just ripe for the picking.

And ready to bruise.

Chapter Two

The wooden deck in front of the cottage overlooked the main house, as well as the fertile vineyard.

Sitting at a glass-topped, wrought-iron table, Sullivan and Lissa enjoyed a stunning view as they shared a glass of wine and watched the sun sink low into the western sky.

"Your sister doesn't look anything like you," Sullivan said by way of small talk. He'd noticed how much Eileen and her mother had resembled each other when they'd brought lunch down to the office.

In fact, Lissa didn't look much like her father, either. Ken Cartwright was short and stocky, with a receding blond hairline and a ruddy complexion. He wasn't much to look at, but he was a hell of a nice guy.

Lissa fingered the stem of her wineglass, as though his comment might have bothered her. And he was sorry he'd brought it up. If he could, he'd reel in the thoughtless words.

She looked up and caught his eye. "I don't look like my family because I'm adopted."

Whoops. He hadn't meant to get so personal. And he wasn't sure how to make up for the klutzy attempt at conversation, so he merely nodded and said, "You've got a nice family."

"Yes, I do." She took a sip of wine. "Do you have any brothers or sisters?"

"Nope. I'm an only child."

"That sounds like it might have been sad growing up."

He shrugged. His childhood had been pretty crappy, but not because he didn't have siblings. "I had a lot of cousins to play with."

"Tell me about your family," she said, settling into the chitchat.

Sullivan rarely talked about himself. Nor about personal matters. But maybe because he'd accidentally prodded the adoption revelation out of her, he felt as though turnaround was fair play.

"My folks both loved me, I guess. But their relationship was stormy, and their marriage ended in divorce before I hit middle school."

"That's too bad."

It was. From an early age, Sullivan had dreamed of belonging to a stable family. Maybe that's why he'd married so early. He'd been ready for kids, picket fences and family vacations. But his wife had refused to consider having his baby, then had left him for another man.

Her leaving had not only dashed his unrealistic dreams and damaged his heart, but it had been a real eye-opening experience. She'd taught him a simple lesson. Sullivan wasn't, and maybe never had been, destined for family life.

"It was no big deal," he lied. "Some people shouldn't ever get married."

"What kind of people?"

Her eyes held a naïveté that surprised him, but he smiled and filled in the blanks as generically as he could. "The kind of people who make promises they don't keep."

His parents' marital nightmare had been brutal for a kid to endure. And his own divorce—six years ago—had been pretty tough.

But hey. He'd bounced back quickly.

His first effort to rebound was by having a few relationships, mostly with shallow socialites who would never tempt him to put his heart on the line again. And it had helped. A lot.

"Funny thing about my folks," he said, wanting to focus his thoughts on his parents' divorce and not his own. "My father's family had money and status. And they could trace their lineage back to the *Mayflower*. But that never seemed to be good enough for my mom."

"Why not?"

He would have shrugged off her question, tried to avoid getting into a conversation that was too deep, one that reminded him of his own failed marriage and was too damn revealing. But for some reason, he cut to the chase. "Some women want more than some men can provide."

She furrowed her brow, but didn't respond. And he wondered whether she had any idea what he was talking about.

Probably not. But that was as far as it would go.

It was bad enough that Sullivan had to relive history in his mind. He didn't need to open himself up to memories best left forgotten.

Lissa wasn't sure what Sullivan meant. And maybe she should ask. But the fact was, they had nothing in common. Nothing on which to build any kind of relationship.

She was adopted and didn't know her biological parents, and he had a lineage tracing back to the *Mayflower*.

He was outgoing and worldly—or so it seemed. And she was as plain and boring as a dust mop.

Still, she was impressed by his business sense and flattered by his charm.

Just then, Barney growled, as though facing a monstrous foe, then began tugging at Sullivan's pant leg.

"Oh, Barney!" Lissa set down her wineglass and

picked up the pesky pooch. "Don't chew on people. That's why you have toys."

Sullivan didn't appear to be bothered by the possibility of a rip or tear in what had to be expensive slacks. "He's a cute little guy. Looks like he has a little collie in him."

She laughed. "And a little beagle and Australian shepherd. In fact, it wouldn't surprise me if he had a bit of dachshund thrown into the mix."

Sullivan chuckled. "He *is* pretty long and close to the ground. Where'd you get him?"

"At the dog pound. His number was up, so I guess you could say I saved his life. They were going to put him to sleep if no one adopted him by the end of that day."

For a moment, Lissa thought about how her parents had chosen her over other orphaned babies.

As a child, she would fantasize about her biological parents, the people who'd given her up. She often thought of them as young lovers, forced apart like Romeo and Juliet.

Once she'd imagined herself as the daughter of royalty, stolen by gypsies and taken to the Children's Connection, where her adoptive parents took pity upon her.

But as she grew older, she put away her childhood fantasies, accepting the fact that her biological parents just hadn't wanted to be bothered with a baby.

Or, more important, that they hadn't wanted to be bothered with *her*.

That didn't, of course, mean that she didn't ever think about them. That she didn't ever wonder who they were or where they lived.

Or whether they ever thought about her.

Jared Cambry sat with his wife behind the closed doors of his home office and studied the telephone he'd just hung up. He glanced at Danielle, who stood beside him, silent and hopeful. Her puffy, red-rimmed eyes undoubtedly mirrored his own.

"What did Dr. Chambers say?" A sense of expectancy lingered in her voice, although her expression reflected the fear and despair they'd been living with since shortly after moving back to Portland.

Jared cleared his throat, trying to break free from the emotion lodged in his chest. "He said that the preliminary tests prove that none of us are a match."

Danielle let out a sob she'd been holding back, and Jared quickly reached her side, taking her in his arms, trying to offer whatever support he could.

"We're going to lose him," she cried. "I feel so helpless."

So did Jared.

Before the diagnosis, their lives had been perfect. Charmed.

He and Danielle were crazy about each other and had a great marriage. They'd thought their family was complete with a son and a daughter. But just eight years ago, they'd been blessed with an unexpected baby they'd named Mark.

Even as an infant, Mark had a joyful heart and a smile that lingered on his lips. He was a loving child, and he soon became the light of their lives.

As Danielle cried, Jared stroked her back, nestled his cheek against the dark-brown curls of her hair. Closed his eyes and blinked back his own tears.

God, this was hard. Brutal.

He held his wife close, trying to share his strength—or maybe to absorb some of hers.

Danielle was an admirable woman. And devoted to her family. At times, he felt as though she was the one who held them all together.

She had teaching credentials—high-school history—but since the birth of their oldest child, she'd been a stay-at-home mom who thrived on being the kind of mother every kid deserved.

Three active children kept her calendar full and her days busy, as she chauffeured them to orthodontic appointments, school events, piano lessons and Little League games. But she still found time to volunteer as a tutor in the adult literacy program at the library.

Jared looked at his wife, unable to tell her everything would be all right. How could he when he didn't know if that was true?

"I'd thought Shawna would be the one," she said. "She and Mark are so much alike."

At fifteen, their daughter promised to be a lovely young woman. But the match could have easily been seventeen-year-old Chad, who was already proving to be a fine athlete, as well as a scholar.

They'd been blessed with three beautiful children. But all of that paled against the stark reality that had rocked their entire world during a youth soccer game.

While playing halfback for the Dragons, eight-year-old Mark had collapsed on the field. Jared had missed the game, since he'd been away on a business trip. But Danielle was there. And she'd rushed Mark to Portland General Hospital, where it was determined the boy had a rare blood disorder.

Without a bone-marrow transplant, their youngest son wouldn't live past the age of ten.

Jared and Danielle had been devastated by the diagnosis but had immediately had the entire family tested as potential donors. Unfortunately, it turned out no one was a match.

"What do we do now?" she asked. "Besides pray that a suitable donor is found in time."

Jared knew there was one last family member out there—somewhere. Someone who might prove to be a match. But finding him or her might be as difficult as finding an unrelated donor in the bone-marrow registry—possible, but against the odds.

"Sit down, Danni," Jared told his wife. "I have something to tell you."

She took a tissue from the wad she'd recently begun to carry in her pocket, wiped her eyes, then sat on the tufted leather seat near the lamp. She didn't say anything. She merely twisted the tissue in her hands and waited for Jared to speak.

"When I was seventeen, I had a one-night stand with a teenaged girl that resulted in pregnancy."

Her brow furrowed, and she looked at him aghast, as though she'd been slapped. "How could you have kept that from me?"

"The girl just disappeared," he said, wishing he'd said something to Danni sooner. They didn't keep secrets from each other. Except for this one, he supposed. But he hadn't known how to tell her, so he'd kept putting it off. "Her name was Olivia. And I'm not sure where she is, or whether she kept the baby or not. But that means we have one more possibility of finding a related match."

His pretty dark-haired wife looked shocked, disappointed and more than a little bit angry. And he couldn't blame her for feeling that way.

"You got a girl pregnant?" she asked. "And you don't even know what she did with the baby?"

"That's the size of it. At this point."

Years ago, Olivia had told him babies were a blessing. Jared hadn't realized she'd been right. Not until Danni had given birth to Chad. And even though he'd been caught up in the miracle of his son's birth, he'd been reminded of his firstborn—a child he'd suggested Olivia abort.

His conscience did a real number on him.

And each time he'd held Danni's hand during the birth of his next two children, thoughts of a faceless newborn came back to haunt him.

Why hadn't he looked for Olivia sooner? He'd intended to.

As the senior attorney in his own corporate law firm with successful offices in several states, Jared had recently moved his family back to Portland, where he'd been born, in order to establish an Oregon-based office.

He'd actually planned to look up Olivia and ask about the baby. And although he didn't usually wade into psychological waters, maybe that was the underlying reason he'd wanted to open the Oregon office himself, rather than send one of his partners. But Jared hadn't gotten a chance to look for her yet.

"When Olivia told me she was pregnant, I offered her money for an abortion, but she refused it. She told me she wanted to keep the baby." Jared rested a hip against the polished, hardwood desk. "When I got settled in the dorms in Phoenix, I called her a couple of times. She was thinking about giving the child up for adoption, which would have been a better idea for her."

"So what did she decide to do?" Danielle asked.

"I'm not sure. I called her again to ask how she was doing and offer her some money." Jared raked a hand through his hair and sighed. "I wasn't working, but I had a small savings account I could drain. Anyway, I pressed her to give the baby up for adoption, which I thought was the best solution. But she flipped out, saying she didn't need my help, then hung up on me."

"And that's how it ended?"

"No. I called her back the next day. Her mother took the message, but Olivia didn't return that call. Or the next one."

"So you just let her go?"

"Not exactly. I figured the baby would be due in the spring, so I called again. But their phone had been disconnected, and there was no forwarding number."

"So how do we go about finding her now?" Danni asked. It seemed that her sense of betrayal had been overcome by her concern for Mark.

"I've got my work cut out for me, but with my investigative skills and enough money to hire the best PI in Oregon, I'll find Olivia and the child."

Jared just hoped he would find them in time.

Dinner around the Cartwright table was a pleasant experience, and Sullivan was glad he'd taken his clients up on the offer to join them.

They dined on grilled filet mignon, tossed salad with an incredible—and undoubtedly homemade—vinaigrette dressing, twice-baked potatoes and a crusty loaf of bread that had filled the house with a warm, yeasty aroma.

Donna Cartwright might be closing in on sixty—or maybe even past it—but she was an attractive woman, with shoulder-length strawberry-blond hair like Eileen's.

And she was a darn good cook. If Sullivan hadn't

already complimented her several times, he'd do so again.

"Tell me," Donna said, resting her elbows on the linen-draped table and eyeing Sullivan with a warm smile. "Where are you from?"

"Originally, I'm from Charleston. But I've been living in Portland for the past five years."

"Oh, really?" She appeared interested. Almost too interested, it seemed. "Does your family still live in Charleston?"

"Yes, they do." His mom and dad kept separate residences in the same prestigious part of town. And in spite of their efforts to avoid each other at all costs, they wouldn't ever move. They had too much invested in the land, the community—the banks.

"That's nice," Donna said. "Why did you choose to move to Oregon?"

Uh-oh. Was she making small talk? Or fishing for information about his marital status and eligibility, like some mothers of single daughters did? After all, she still had one more to marry off.

He ought to give Donna the benefit of the doubt, but he couldn't help staying on his toes, ready to make a mad dash for cover. "I moved to Portland for business reasons." *His* business—and nobody else's.

If Sullivan had to see his ex-wife on Gregory Atwater's arm at one more society function, he might have done something to embarrass himself. It had been tough enough living down the fiasco that sent his parents' marriage spiraling into court, so as soon as his divorce had become final, he'd gotten the hell out of Charleston. And five years later, here he was. He'd moved practically from one corner of the United States to another.

Could he have gotten any farther away from his ex or his war-torn childhood?

"Portland is a nice city," Donna said.

Sullivan nodded. "I like it."

Her blue eyes sparkled in a doting mama way, and any red-blooded single man could see her cogs and wheels turning, could sense her maternal game plan. So he braced himself for another round of the bachelor two-step, a defensive move he'd quickly mastered.

He took a sip of wine and savored the taste of the Valencia merlot that was every bit as good as Ken and Lissa had told him it was.

"Are you married?" Donna asked.

Ah, he'd been right. The tenacious woman had finally gone for the jugular. Fortunately, he'd become adept at maintaining his privacy and his happy-go-lucky bachelor status. "No, I'm not married."

"It must be lonely for you."

Lissa, who'd just lifted her wineglass for a sip, choked momentarily, then pressed a white linen napkin to her mouth before saying, "Excuse me."

Sullivan stole a glance her way and realized she wasn't at all comfortable with her mother's shift to yenta mode. He sympathized with the young woman who probably was as happy to be unattached as he was. If she weren't, he suspected she'd dress differently.

"I enjoy the freedom to come and go as I choose," he told the mother.

"Well, that's wonderful," Donna said, although Sullivan had a feeling she thought it was wonderful that he was a bachelor. And that she'd quickly put aside the fact he liked being single.

The older woman tucked a wavy strand of shoulder-length hair behind her ear and continued to hone in on her target. "Surely a man like you must be seeing someone special."

Sullivan had been down this road many times before. "I date several ladies, Mrs. Cartwright. And each of them is pretty special."

"You'll have to forgive my wife for prying into your life," Ken said, with a chuckle. "She thinks everyone needs to be as happily married as we are."

Yeah, well Sullivan's experience told him that many women liked to play matchmaker, whether they were happily married or not.

For some reason, the female of the species seemed to harbor a happily-ever-after fantasy, but he didn't hold on to that illusion any longer. Katherine and Clarence Grayson might have been proper and genteel when they socialized with Charleston's wealthy families. But behind the walls of the family estate, they hadn't behaved any differently than a warring couple in the seedier part of town. The broken dishes and figurines merely cost more money to replace.

''I'm afraid growing up in the midst of marital misery has made me gun-shy,'' Sullivan said.

Donna seemed to take his statement into consideration and didn't immediately speak.

Sullivan slid a glance at Lissa, who sat up straight—much like a rocket ready to blast off. She probably needed a break as badly as he did.

He shifted in his seat toward Ken, intending to send the conversation in a safer direction, and caught the vintner's eyes. ''This merlot is excellent. I think we'll need to work the marketing strategy around it, too.''

''I thought you'd like it.'' The older man leaned back in his chair. ''But you haven't tasted anything until you try Lissa's new blend.''

''I'm looking forward to it.'' This time, when Sullivan glanced at Lissa, she didn't seem to be quite as tense. Maybe more like a firecracker than a rocket.

He didn't usually sympathize with single women whose mothers were dead set on seeing them in white lace and a veil, but shy and unassuming Lissa tugged at a sympathetic vein in his heart.

Besides, from what he'd learned while researching his new clients, Lissa loved the vineyard and had a real head for business. The people he'd spoken to referred to her as a career woman, with nothing on her mind but the success of the family vineyard.

And that assessment had been validated by what he'd observed earlier today. He figured she meant to make Valencia Vineyards her life.

Apparently, her mother hadn't wanted to accept that decision.

"Can I get anyone seconds?" Donna asked.

"Not me." Sullivan leaned away from the table. "I haven't eaten this well in ages."

Again, he looked at Lissa, who seemed to be studying her plate. Unless she'd gotten a full heaping of seconds when he wasn't looking, she hadn't eaten much at all. He had a feeling the mother-hen inquisition had annoyed her, too.

And why shouldn't it bother her? She had a business relationship with Sullivan to think about. And they had a lot of work ahead of them. Romantic thoughts would only get in the way, distract them from their focus.

As soon as he could get her alone, he'd have to let her know that this stuff happened to him all the time, and that she shouldn't be the least bit embarrassed, not on his account.

"Decaffeinated coffee anyone?" Donna asked, obviously in her element as a gracious hostess.

"I'll have a cup," Ken said.

The attractive older woman tossed Sullivan a pleasant smile. "How about you?"

"No thank you." Sullivan was ready for the evening to end, especially since he wasn't about to lay himself open for any more questions. And he didn't particularly like seeing Lissa look as if she were sitting in a dental chair, waiting for a root canal.

The dark-haired young woman gathered her nearly

full plate and silverware, along with those of her father and Sullivan, then went into the kitchen, followed by her mother.

Minutes later, when they returned with coffee and slices of cheesecake with a raspberry sauce, Donna wore a solemn expression.

Had she been chastised by her daughter? Probably so, because Lissa looked a bit more comfortable than when she'd been seated at the table.

No telling what—if anything—had gone on in the kitchen, but Sullivan had a feeling Lissa had asked her mother to back off. He hoped the older woman's curiosity had been sated. For everyone's sake.

Actually, Donna Cartwright was a nice lady. Just determined to marry off her last daughter, he supposed.

But Sullivan wasn't in the market for a wife. Not now. Not ever. And the sooner the Cartwrights understood that, the better.

Lissa couldn't wait for the horrible evening to end. What must Sullivan think of her—or her mother?

She knew her mom didn't mean any harm, but if Lissa ever decided to go on a manhunt, she didn't want her mother to pave the way.

At least after their little chat in the kitchen, Mom had gotten the message that Lissa wasn't looking for a husband.

Of course, if she'd been more like Eileen, Sullivan Grayson would have made a great catch. But she wasn't anything like Eileen. And besides, he'd made himself clear. He was happy being a bachelor.

"The cheesecake was delicious," Sullivan said. "In fact, the entire meal was out of this world. I'm going to put on weight while I work here."

Donna beamed like a Girl Scout with a new merit badge. "Well, I'm glad you decided to join us."

Relieved to see the stressful dinner conversation winding down, Lissa pushed her seat away from the table. "If you don't mind, I'll slip into the kitchen and wash the dishes."

Sullivan stood and reached for his desert plate and fork. "Let me help you."

Lissa nearly dropped the cup and saucer she'd picked up, but for the life of her, she couldn't speak, couldn't object. Of course, knowing her mother, she wouldn't have to.

"How thoughtful," Donna told Sullivan, even though it was her habit to shoo off any guest who volunteered to help in the kitchen. "Ken and I will just go on to bed."

At seven-thirty?

Ken glanced at his watch, furrowed his brow, then cocked his head. "It's pretty early for bed, don't you think?"

Lissa didn't take time to listen to her mother's explanation. Instead, she disappeared into the kitchen.

Unfortunately, Sullivan followed her.

She wanted to tell him that she needed some time

alone, to regroup after her mother's lame attempt to find her a husband. But she kept her mouth shut for a while, until she could figure out what to say.

"I noticed how uncomfortable you were in there," he said.

Lissa stood at the sink, her hand frozen on the faucet, warm water flowing from the spigot.

"But don't let it get to you," he said. "I'm used to that kind of thing."

What kind of thing was that? Mothers who tried to find husbands for their spinster daughters?

For goodness' sake. Even if Lissa had been willing to accept her mother's help, the least her mom could do was find a man who actually wanted to settle down.

She turned around to face him, catching a whiff of his taunting highland scent and falling into his hazel gaze. Her heart skipped a beat, and she tried desperately to hide her feelings, her insecurities, all of those things that had worked against her since meeting Sullivan.

"Just so you know," she said, "I have no plans to get married. Ever."

Okay, so she lied. Sort of. She had dreams, of course, enhanced by the stack of romances on her nightstand. But no *plans*. She knew better than to believe a frog could turn into a princess.

"I had a feeling you felt the same way I do," Sullivan said. "Don't you hate it when people try to screw up our contentment?"

She nodded, even though she wasn't all that contented. But at least she didn't have to deal with embarrassment.

Sullivan slid her a crooked smile that made her knees go weak. What an interesting mouth he had.

A mouth that undoubtedly knew how to kiss a woman.

Milt Preston had kissed her once, after their date to the Christmas formal. Lissa had actually been looking forward to it, since Eileen had told her about making out with Jason Crowley in the back seat of his Mustang.

But her first kiss hadn't been anything like her sister's romantic experience. In fact, it had been just plain awful.

Instead of taking it slow and easy, Milt had opened his mouth and zeroed in on her, slapping a wet tongue across her lips, trying to poke and prod his way inside her mouth. She'd pushed him away, but the kiss had left her feeling dirty, sticky and wet.

Disgusted and disappointed, she'd left him standing on the porch and escaped inside the house, where she dashed upstairs to brush her teeth and rid herself of his taste.

Her efforts hadn't worked, so she'd tried a shower. But not even hot, sudsy water could wash away the yucky memory.

As Sullivan squeezed a squirt of dish soap into the sink, his presence closed in on her. The side of his arm brushed against her shoulder, leaving a warm tingle after he moved away. "Would you like to wash or dry?"

"It doesn't matter," she said, trying to focus on the mundane household task. "Which would you rather do?"

"Since I don't know where anything goes, I'll wash."

As the soap formed a frothy foam, Lissa's thoughts drifted from the kitchen sink to a bubble bath in a candlelit bathroom. She'd read a book once where the hero and heroine had showered together, lathering each other until their passion blazed.

Oh, for Pete's sake. She was letting her imagination and her hormones get the best of her.

Sullivan handed her a rinsed plate, and she quickly wiped it dry. They didn't talk much, and before long, the kitchen was back in order.

"I'll see you tomorrow morning," he said, before leaving her alone with her thoughts.

Or rather with her adolescent hormones raging.

What would she have done if the guy had actually come on to her?

She would have skedaddled like a scaredy cat, no doubt.

But Lissa couldn't help wondering what Sullivan's kiss would be like. She had a feeling she might like to let his tongue inside her mouth, but she shrugged off the possibility. A woman like her knew better than to dwell on an impossible dream.

Or to dwell on a handsome bachelor with a playful smile and more than his fair share of pheromones.

Chapter Three

At nine the next morning, Sullivan met Lissa at the vineyard office, a small, wood-paneled room that held file cabinets, a computer and an expansive antique desk. It looked like the usual workplace, but a mauve, overstuffed sofa against the far wall and a kitchenette in the corner suggested Lissa spent a lot of time here.

And so did the little puppy that lay curled up on a doggie bed by the potbellied stove.

Sullivan watched as Lissa made a pot of coffee from beans she'd ground only a moment ago.

As she had yesterday, she wore a plain, loose-fitting blouse and the same style of baggy trousers—this time a drab brown.

Why did she choose such dull colors when green or blue would highlight those expressive eyes?

Her mother and sister dressed stylishly, so he had to assume that Lissa preferred to be nondescript. Was that so she would be taken more seriously in the business world? Maybe. It made sense.

As she worked, he watched her from behind. She'd woven her hair into a long, single braid that hung down her back. He figured the strands might reach her waist, if she let it free.

Lissa turned, facing him. "How do you like your coffee?"

"Sugar," he said. "No cream."

He'd expected her to turn around and return to her work, but she didn't move. She just stood there like a deer in the meadow, head raised, eyes focused on a potential foe.

"What are you looking at?" she asked.

"Nothing." He hadn't meant to be gawking. But long hair on women had always fascinated him.

If he and Lissa were dating, and his opinion meant something to her, he'd suggest she wear it loose, over her shoulders and down her back. But they weren't dating, so he kept his opinion to himself.

Still, he had half a notion to tease her a bit, to see if she would loosen up. He was flirtatious by nature, and the playful banter between a man and a woman came easily to him. But he'd better back off. His relationship with Lissa was strictly business. And he'd be wise to keep it that way.

The coffee began to gurgle and sputter as it dribbled into the pot, and soon, the aroma of a robust brew permeated the room.

Lissa withdrew a crystal sugar bowl and two mugs from the small overhead cupboard, and he watched the braid swish along the curve of her back. Yesterday she'd worn her hair twisted in a knot. Did she prefer it trussed up and out of the way?

Maybe she disliked it long, but was too busy to go to the salon for a cut and style. It didn't matter, he supposed. But the woman intrigued him for some reason.

Her shyness maybe? Her focus on business and finances? Or maybe because he suspected there was a lot more going on behind those vibrant green eyes than most people knew.

As she handed him a cup of coffee, their fingers brushed, and something passed between them. A soft and gentle awareness, a lingering connection of some kind.

Had that initial little spark of attraction he'd felt for her grown?

If so, he wouldn't act upon it. Lissa Cartwright was too complex, too real. Too rooted in family and responsibility. When he'd been younger and more naive, she would have been the kind of woman he could have cared for—before he'd learned not to believe in romantic dreams.

She snagged his gaze. "Did anyone ever tell you that you have the most interesting eyes?"

He had interesting eyes? Hell, she was the one with

eyes that would stop a man dead in his tracks. But he didn't want to go there.

"My eyes aren't anything special," he said. "They're just brown—or hazel, I guess."

"The sunlight is coming through that window." She nodded to the pane of glass on the east wall. "And it highlights little gold flecks. The color is really unusual."

Sullivan stiffened. He wasn't comfortable with her looking at him like that, as if he had something she'd never seen before, as if she thought he was someone special. But he quickly scoffed it off.

She'd only noticed his eye color because of the way the morning sun poured through the window. And she'd merely made a comment, which for some goofy reason, he continued to ponder.

Did his eyes really have gold flecks? If he had a mirror handy, he'd take a peek, just to see what she saw.

"The color is beautiful," she said, her voice going kind of soft.

"Just in the sunlight." He cast off her compliment and tried to shift the focus away from himself. "You're the one with a stunning pair of peepers."

She cocked her head slightly, as though trying to decipher his words. "Me?"

"What's the matter? Surely, you've had tons of compliments over the years."

"Mostly from my mom," she said, cheeks starting

to flush. "Although maybe some lady in a grocery store said something once or twice."

Well, now. See? *That's* what happened when a person tried to downplay their looks so no one would notice them. Sometimes it worked.

"You do have pretty eyes," he told her. "Whether you believe it or not. They're the color of new leaves."

Great. Now he was talking like a friggin' poet.

She thanked him, yet still appeared skeptical.

"By the way," he added, reneging on his earlier decision to keep his opinion to himself. "You ought to wear green or blue. To bring out the color of your eyes, you know."

She glanced down at a pair of brown, rubber-soled loafers—shoes that looked a lot like the ones his great-aunt Clara wore. Then she looked up at him with a doe-eyed gaze that reached deep into his chest.

Whoa. That was a little too close for comfort.

He took his mug, then turned and strode toward the sofa—but only because it was on the far side of the room. Away from her, away from the weird stuff he felt whenever she looked at him that way.

Lissa Cartwright was *not* the kind of woman he pursued. And she was certainly off-limits until his business with the vineyard was over.

From across the room, and from a much safer distance, he turned, took a sip of coffee then asked, "How about a tour of the vineyard?"

"Sure. After we go over the guest list for the dinner

party tomorrow night. I'd like you to know who'll be there ahead of time." Lissa reached into the top desk drawer, withdrew a sheet of paper and set it upon the oak desktop.

"What's the purpose of the gathering?" he asked.

"We want to start a buzz about the new blend. So we've invited several local vintners and a reporter from *Through the Grapevine,* a local magazine that has expanded its circulation and should bring in more tourists and interest in the wine region."

While Lissa described each guest and gave Sullivan a rundown of their holdings and achievements in the industry, they finished their coffee. Then, leaving the puppy to snooze on its bed, they set out to see every nook and cranny of the vineyard.

The air was fresh and clean from a rain they'd had a couple days before, and as they strolled through the parklike grounds, Sullivan was amazed at the beauty of the place. Besides row upon row of grapes that grew on the rolling hillsides, the lush property displayed a stone-lined fishpond that hosted several mallards and two black swans.

The manicured lawns nearly begged for people to sit and relish the peaceful sight.

"Why haven't you opened up Valencia Vineyards for visitors and tastings?" he asked. "The grounds are beautiful, and I think you could really draw in a fair number of tourists each month."

"We've thought about it," Lissa said. "But we've always preferred our privacy."

"You called me in for advice," he reminded her.

"And my father and I intend to consider everything you suggest." She led him into the new winery that had replaced the older facility they'd used in the past.

"The construction of this building was a major expense," she explained. "And some hidden costs depleted our funds more than we're comfortable with. That's the primary reason we brought you in as a marketing consultant."

"Then you're in luck. I'm always glad to offer my services."

She bit her bottom lip and looked at him out of the corner of her eye. She wore an interesting expression.

One that seemed to ask how far he'd go to offer his services.

After they'd explored the new winery, Sullivan said, "You've done a wonderful job creating a modern and efficient operation."

Lissa thought so, too. "Thank you."

"And if you decide to open the vineyard and winery for tours, word will quickly spread."

"You're probably right." She'd have to discuss it with her father. After all, he was the one who valued his privacy.

"So, where's that killer new blend I've been hearing about?" Sullivan asked. "Do I have to wait for that dinner party tomorrow night?"

"No. I can let you have a taste now."

"Great." He flashed her a smile that made her

heart skip a beat, which was surprising, since she'd grown a lot more comfortable with the man over the past few hours.

Lissa led him to the tasting room, then took two glasses from the stash they kept in a solid oak cabinet. The walls were lined with wine bottles tucked into crisscrossed shelves. But her special blend remained in an oak barrel that appeared to be only a decoration. She pulled the tap, filled both glasses and offered one to Sullivan.

Before taking a drink, he clinked his goblet against hers and offered a toast. "To the special lady who made this wine."

Lissa appreciated his thoughtful gesture, but didn't take a sip. Instead, she watched for Sullivan's reaction, studying the good-looking man over the rim of her glass.

She guessed he was a bit of a playboy. But how could he not be, with those sexy eyes and that flirty smile?

Sullivan Grayson was too darn attractive for his own good. Or rather, for her own good.

Yet he also had a wealth of sexual experience and could make a woman's first time special. At least, she suspected he would.

If Lissa had any courage at all, she'd suggest a brief affair. After all, who would get hurt? Not her. She had no illusions about falling in love.

And he certainly wouldn't get hurt, since he'd probably never given a thought to settling down. Besides, once his job with Valencia Vineyards was finished, he'd be on his way. And that reason, on top of her fierce attraction, made him a perfect first-time lover—if she were inclined to act out the silly fantasy.

For Pete's sake. What if he wasn't the least bit interested in being her one-time lover? And if he were, her attempts to please him would be clumsy at best. Either way, she'd be embarrassed. Humiliated.

Mortified.

Fortunately, she was too shy to even suggest it.

Sullivan closed his eyes and appeared to be savoring the taste of the wine.

She held her breath, waiting for him to comment.

When his gaze locked on hers, his expression grew serious. "Lissa, this is incredible. I'm no expert, by any means, but I know what I like."

She blew out the breath she'd been holding. "Really?"

"It's great." His eyes verified his sincerity. "With the fresh, unique taste we'll need a name, something that will reflect the newness, as well as the appeal."

"I agree." Both she and her dad hoped that the wine would increase sales—with the right marketing strategy. "Any ideas?"

He thought for a while, then broke into a lazy grin. "There's one word we need to use in the name."

"What's that?" She took a sip from her glass.

"Virgin."

Virgin? Lissa choked, sputtered and coughed.

"Are you okay?"

She cleared her throat. "I'm fine. I guess it just went down the wrong pipe."

The explanation seemed to appease him, although she really hadn't swallowed wrong. His comment had surprised her. Heck, the way Sullivan said *virgin* made it seem as though he thought virginity held some kind of merit, some value.

If that were the case, maybe her inexperience wouldn't scare him away.

The idea of losing her innocence to Sullivan made her imagination soar. Of course, he'd probably be shocked if she suggested it—assuming she had the nerve to broach the subject. After all, she'd never been suggestive or forward—sexually speaking.

Besides, Sullivan had his share of beautiful women. What would make him settle for a nobody like her?

She could, of course, dream. Couldn't she?

Lissa had become good at fantasizing. Which certainly helped, because the thought of going to her deathbed as a virgin was downright depressing, if she dwelled upon it.

"Virgin Mist," he said. "Now, *that's* a name that would appeal to the masses. It promises something new and fresh. What do you think?"

Before she could tell him it worked for her, the big, oval-topped door opened, and her father walked into the tasting room.

"How'd you like the tour?" he asked Sullivan.

"It was great. Enlightening. And the tour director

really knows her stuff.'' Sullivan shot Lissa a smile that nearly wobbled her knees.

''Well, she ought to. Lissa loves the vineyard.'' Ken slid an arm around her shoulder and gave her a squeeze. ''In fact, she's the daughter who takes after me.''

Sullivan chuckled, and Lissa smiled.

It was nice when her father said things like that, when he seemed to forget that she was adopted.

But they both knew there was another man out there—somewhere. A faceless man who could actually lay claim to her genetic makeup.

In his Portland law office, Jared studied a legal brief, yet his mind wasn't on his work.

He was still reeling over the fact that the clock was ticking. That he still didn't know anything about Olivia Maddison or her child. That the PI he'd hired had been due to check in ten minutes ago.

Just as he glanced at his gold wristwatch, a beep sounded over the intercom system.

''Mr. Cambry?'' his secretary asked.

''Yes.''

''Mr. Hastings with Investigative Specialties is here to see you.''

''Send him in.'' Jared was eager to know what the investigator had learned, whether he'd found Olivia yet.

Moments later, Sam Hastings entered. He was a big

man with a full head of blond hair and prominent brows that shaded pensive eyes.

Jared stood and reached across the table to shake hands. "Any news?"

"Yeah. I'm afraid so." Sam blew out a sigh. "Olivia is dead."

Dead? Jared slowly dropped to his seat. "What happened?"

"Car accident. Twenty-seven years ago."

"And the baby?" Jared asked, heart pounding. Had the child died, too?

"It was made a ward of the state and put up for adoption."

"Now what?" Jared asked.

"Well, let me tell you what I've learned, what we've got to work with." Sam took the seat in front of the desk, as though the revelation might take a while. "Olivia and her mother were involved in a traffic accident. Mrs. Maddison was killed instantly, and Olivia was critically injured. Paramedics took her to Portland General Hospital, where she remained in a coma until she died a few weeks later."

"So, what do the hospital records show?" Jared asked.

"That's the problem." Sam took a deep breath, then slowly let it out. "A few months after Olivia's death, a severe storm caused a power surge through-out the county. The hospital's backup generator kicked on a few seconds later, and the patients were okay. But because the computers are old and the hospital birth clinic lacked funding until the new owners, the Logans, came on board, the computer files were either lost or are nearly impossible to retrieve.''

''But surely there are paper files, not just the computer entries,'' Jared said, hoping his efforts to find his firstborn hadn't struck out completely.

''I'm afraid not. When the power surged, it caused a circuit breaker in the clinic to spark. Some of the sparks landed on a cutesy wall hanging they used as a nursery decoration. A fire started, eliminating a number of paper files regarding adoptions, foster care situations, fertility information and other things.''

Jared could hear his pulse pounding in his ears, could feel his palms growing moist, his stomach knotting. ''Are you telling me that we can't find out what happened to the baby?''

''The child survived the accident, was born prematurely and put up for adoption through the Children's Connection. What we've got are bits and pieces of information.''

''Like what?'' Jared asked, his hopes resurrecting.

''A name, an address, a gender…but I'm not sure what matches up.''

''Let's see what you've got, and we'll take it from there.''

Could that baby he'd fathered twenty-seven years ago be the miracle they needed?

That evening, as Lissa prepared for bed, she couldn't find Barney. And when she asked her folks, neither of them had seen him, either. Obviously, the rascally pup had sneaked out again. But it was too dangerous for him to stay outside all night.

She grabbed her robe and put on a pair of slippers, intent on searching the grounds.

As she stood on the front porch and scanned the lawn and the pond, she spotted Sullivan sitting quietly on the deck of the cottage, her puppy in his lap.

"Looking for this little guy?" he called out.

"Yes." She touched the sash of her blue chenille robe, checking to see that it was snug, then fingered the edge of the lapel, making sure it covered her flannel nightgown.

She walked across the grass, then made her way over the small, wooden bridge.

All the while, Sullivan watched her.

She felt weird letting him see her like this, yet she was probably more bundled up than in her street clothes.

When she neared the guest cottage, he asked, "Why don't you join me for a while?"

Join him? Sit down on one of the padded, wrought-iron chairs on the wooden porch and chat? She really ought to take Barney and go back to the house, yet something urged her to stay.

"All right," she said. "Just for a few minutes."

He glanced into his lap, where the puppy rested. "This little rascal was chasing a duck, who didn't take too kindly to being barked at."

Lissa laughed. "Barney has a lot to learn."

"But he's brave. Instead of running back to the house with his tail between his legs, he wandered over to me."

"You were sitting out here?"

He nodded. "I like sitting outside when the day is done."

She didn't tell him, since it seemed like an insignificant thing for two people to have in common, that sitting on the deck in the backyard was how she always started her days.

"My great-aunt Clara has a front porch like this. It overlooks the stream that runs through her property." Sullivan shot her a crooked grin. "You have a lot in common with her."

"How so?"

He shook his head and chuckled, but didn't answer.

For some reason, she had a feeling he wasn't being complimentary. And that the commonality she shared with his aunt wasn't something to be proud of. But curiosity got the better of her. "Speak up, or I'll take my dog and go home."

His eyes crinkled with mirth. "She wears comfortable walking shoes like yours. And she wraps herself in chenille and flannel before going to sleep."

So, Lissa had been right. He *was* making fun of her. Yet there wasn't a cruel edge to his laughter. And she chose not to be offended by his teasing. Heck, there was nothing wrong with choosing comfort over glamour and style.

"What would you prefer I wear?" she asked. "Stiletto heels and a silk scarf?"

His eyes lit up. "Do you have them hidden in your bedroom?"

She swatted at his arm. "No. But I've got drawers full of flannel and chenille."

"Too bad." He slid her a playful grin.

The conversation had turned a bit sexual, which might have excited her, had she been dressed in satin. But her chenille robe weighed heavily upon her shoulders.

"Well," she said. "Those few minutes have flown by. And it's time for me to turn in."

"I hope you're not mad. Great-aunt Clara is a great gal. And she's got more spunk than her eighty-five-year-old sister."

Lissa arched a brow. "How old is your aunt?"

"Ninety-seven. And she still mows her own yard and works in the garden."

"Impressive. Then there's hope for the flannel-and-chenille crowd."

"Great-aunt Clara has a boyfriend, too." He tossed her a dimpled grin.

"You don't say." Lissa figured she'd be ninety before a guy noticed her.

She glanced toward the house and saw that her parents had turned off their bedroom light. Her mother's doing, no doubt. Trying to give Lissa a little push toward romance.

When she looked at Sullivan, he was gazing at her.

"Are you involved with anyone?" he asked.

The question took her aback—in part because the truth was too revealing. She didn't mind if he knew she chose sensible shoes. Or that she wore flannel to bed. But she didn't want him to think of her as the awkward virgin that she was.

So she said, "No one at the moment."

He didn't comment, merely studied her.

But she was afraid he'd see through her half truth, so she stood. "Well, I really need to go. Don't let the bed bugs bite."

He stroked Barney's head. "I'll see you in the morning."

She nodded, then reached to pick up the sleeping pup. As she did so, their hands touched, and a warm shiver shimmied through her veins.

Before she could react—or run—Sullivan tugged gently upon her braid. "Do you ever let your hair down, Lissa?"

"Never," she said, her voice a near whisper.

"You ought to." His words settled over her like a cloak of crushed velvet.

She slowly straightened, pulling her braid from his hand. "Good night. I'll see you in the morning."

As she strode toward the house, she tried to shake the adolescent fascination with a man who was out of her league.

Yet she couldn't shake the thought of letting her hair down—for him.

Chapter Four

Do you ever let your hair down?

Lissa stood before the antique floor-length mirror in her bedroom, studying the brown mop that hung over her shoulders and down her back.

Why didn't she just go to the salon in town and have it all chopped off?

Because she'd become so good at braiding it, so used to twisting it this way or that. Shorter hair meant styling gel, mousse, curling irons and spray—stuff Lissa had never been adept at using. Of course, she could always plop a hat on her head.

But not on a special occasion like tonight.

She'd dressed in a black, A-line dress with three-quarter length sleeves and a hem that reached midcalf. The simple style suited her.

Now, the only thing left to do was her hair. For a moment, she considered letting it hang loose—as Sullivan had suggested. But she felt incomplete, exposed. And far too vulnerable for a night like this.

Her dad planned to serve the new blend Lissa had created as a prelude to a bigger unveiling later this month. But with the exclusive guest list of local vintners and wine connoisseurs, Lissa felt this dinner party was critical and her nerves were on edge.

And to add more stress to the evening, her dad had invited that reporter from *Through the Grapevine* magazine to record everyone's reaction.

Normally, Lissa preferred to blend into the crowd, to be discreet and unnoticed. But her basic shyness didn't surface while she was making wine or discussing the vineyard she loved. So, for the first time in years, Lissa had actually primped—a little.

She decided upon a French braid that hung down her back. The style might be a bit more elegant than she was used to, but tonight called for something special, out of the ordinary.

If Eileen were here, she'd insist Lissa put on some makeup. A while back, her sister had given her a monstrous palette of colorful goop for no reason at all, volunteering to help her choose the perfect shades. Unfortunately, Lissa had declined the lesson.

She glanced at the unused palette that sat on the bathroom counter. As klutzy as she was, she'd probably smear on the stuff and look like a clown. Yet a tiny spark of vanity surfaced, and she picked up a tube of lipstick, lifted the lid and rolled out the stick. A pink gloss. She could handle something simple like that.

And what was in this blue tube? Mascara? Maybe a dab would be okay. She unscrewed the top and pulled out the small, curved brush. Leaning toward the bathroom mirror, she stroked the bristles along her lashes.

Gosh, this was tough. And some women fussed with makeup every day. Talk about gluttons for punishment.

Her mouth opened on its own, which seemed to help with her aim. Maybe a little to the left.

Ow! Damn. Right in the eyeball. Ouch. And it stung. By the time she rubbed and blinked, two black smears made her look like a raccoon.

Forget it. Vanity was definitely overrated.

Somehow, she managed to get her face washed, but her eyes still looked a bit dark around the edges. Well, that's what she got for trying to be somebody else— somebody feminine and attractive.

She looked at her watch. Six forty-five. Oh shoot. People would be arriving any minute. She slipped on a pair of low-heeled black pumps—sensible shoes like good old Aunt Clara wore, she supposed—then headed for the kitchen to give her mother a hand.

Donna had hired a caterer for this evening, so there probably wasn't much left for Lissa to do, other than greet everyone.

Just as she stepped away from the foot of the stairs,

a knock sounded, alerting her to the arrival of the first guest. Showtime. She strode across the carpet to the polished hardwood entry and opened the door.

Sullivan stood on the porch, wearing expensive-looking black slacks, a white shirt—open at the collar—and a stylish sports jacket. A *GQ* cover boy come to life.

He flashed her a playful grin. "You look great this evening, Lissa. Nice dress."

"Thank you." Did he really think she looked nice? Or was that just the standard how-do-you-do comment that folks made at dinner parties?

"You did something to your eyes," he said.

"Yeah. During a moment of weakness, I nearly blinded myself. But it won't happen again. Come on inside." She stepped away from the door and led him through the living room. "Can I get you a drink?"

"How about Scotch and water?"

"You've got it."

Within moments, the house began to fill with the local vintners and wine connoisseurs they'd invited. Lissa milled around, making cocktail-hour conversation.

The next doorbell announced the arrival of the last guest, or so Lissa hoped. The reporter from *Through the Grapevine* magazine had yet to arrive.

Her name was Gretchen, which was all Lissa had been told over the telephone. No one had prepared Lissa for the voluptuous blonde in a traffic-stopping red dress revealed when the door swung open.

The word *tacky* came to mind, but that wasn't really true. The blonde merely had a sophisticated style and a healthy dose of self-confidence.

But heck, Lissa would feel confident, too—if she had a face and figure like that.

More than a few men turned to gawk, as the statuesque woman stepped into the foyer. Unable to help herself, Lissa peeked at the woman's feet, expecting to see high heels. Wow. Those red strappy sandals weren't exactly stilettos, but they were pretty darn close. They also showed off a pedicure and cherry-red toenail polish.

Lissa glanced at her own size nines. At least the dependable pumps were comfortable. And who needed bunions and foot problems later on? Heck, Sullivan's Great-aunt Clara probably had gorgeous feet—wrinkled, maybe. But not all crippled up from years of abuse.

Gathering the hostess skills her mom had taught her, Lissa extended a hand and introduced herself to the attractive reporter. "You must be Gretchen Thomas."

"Yes, I am. Thank you for inviting me." Gretchen's lively blue eyes quickly scanned the milling crowd, then landed on Sullivan.

And wouldn't you know it? The sexy *GQ* hottie had spotted her, too.

"Who's that man near the bookcase?" Gretchen asked. "Is he one of the local vintners? I don't believe I've met him."

"He's a business consultant," Lissa said.

"Interesting."

Yes, wasn't it? Lissa wanted to place the sole of her sensible shoe on the blonde's shapely backside and boot her out of the house before the reporter and the consultant had a chance to exchange telephone numbers.

But why bother?

Lissa didn't need a crystal ball or a cup of tea leaves to see how the evening would unfold. She could sense what was coming down the pike.

Well, *c'est la vie.*

Here today. Gone tomorrow.

Que sera, sera.

With hormones dancing in her eyes, Gretchen threw back her shoulders, lifted her chin and made her way toward the only eligible bachelor in the room. Well, the only bachelor in the twenty- to forty-something range.

One of their guests, Anthony Martinelli, a longtime friend of her father's and a successful local vintner, had lost his wife last winter. Rumor had it he was looking to find love again. But the older man, while handsome, was probably too tame for a woman like Gretchen.

On the other hand, Sullivan was more the reporter's style. And the lady in red appeared to have staked her claim.

So much for Lissa's silly hope of having a one-time fling with the consultant. She had a feeling Sullivan would be taken before the night was over.

But why should she give a flying leap about that? She'd known nothing would ever become of her silly fantasy. Still, as she watched Sullivan smile at the blonde's swivel-hipped approach, an ache settled in her chest.

Get over it, she told herself, shoving aside the sting of disappointment and hiding behind an I'm-not-the-least-bit-interested stance.

Anthony Martinelli approached her little corner of the world, interrupting her thoughts.

"Hello, Lissa." The handsome older man, who wore his Italian heritage well, flashed her a charming smile that crinkled along the edges of his sharp blue eyes. "You look lovely tonight."

Lissa didn't warrant the "lovely" comment, although she had tried to look her best this evening. But she appreciated Anthony's kindness, especially as she watched her hopeless romantic fantasy go up in a sensuous swirl of smoke. "Thank you. You look rather dashing yourself."

Anthony must have been a real lady-killer when he was younger, because he was one of the most attractive middle-aged men she knew. Many of her father's friends and business associates developed a paunch, a softness. But the widowed vintner didn't appear to have aged in all the years Lissa had known him.

The silver at his temples merely gave him added charm, while a trim, solid physique and a sun-deepened olive complexion suggested he still did a lot of the physical work on his vineyard.

"I hear you're about to introduce a new blend this evening," Anthony said.

Lissa smiled, glad to focus on her work. "We're calling it Virgin Mist."

"Sounds intriguing. And appealing."

So Sullivan had been right. The name was perfect in a marketing sense.

"We wanted our closest friends to be the first to taste it," she added.

"Then I'm especially happy you've included me." Anthony cast her a charming Al Pacino smile. "I've been meaning to call you, Lissa. I'm not sure what your calendar looks like, but I'd like to take you to lunch or dinner someday soon."

The comment took her aback. Had the widowed vintner taken an interest in her?

A romantic interest?

Surely not. He probably wanted to discuss business.

"I'll have to check my calendar, but since my dad is leaving for San Diego in the next day or so, I'll be pretty busy."

"What's in San Diego?"

"He needs to get his uncle situated in an intermediate-care facility." She didn't want Anthony thinking she was trying to blow him off, so she added, "While Dad's gone, I'll be working with the marketing consultant we brought in, but after he goes home, I should have some time.''

''Good. I'll give you a call next week,'' Anthony said, his blue eyes vivid and…

And what?

Flirtatious?

Not likely. Ever since Sullivan had arrived on the scene, Lissa's schoolgirl imagination had certainly taken her on a romantic joy ride.

Still, she liked the idea that someone might have found her attractive—even if he was more than twenty years her senior.

Gretchen Thomas had latched on to Sullivan for the cocktail hour and it appeared she planned to stay that way until after breakfast tomorrow morning.

She was an attractive woman, aware of her beauty and adept at showing off her double-D assets to the fullest. Sullivan might have taken her up on the unspoken offer of sex, had they met while he was on vacation. But his only interest in Gretchen this evening was the article she would write about Virgin Mist.

Her lips curled into a smile. ''Maybe we can sit together during dinner.''

''Mrs. Cartwright has probably assigned place settings.'' At least Sullivan hoped so. It would make things easier for him if Gretchen latched on to someone else for the remainder of the evening. Otherwise, he'd have to make sure he rejected her affections with grace and charm. If he failed to do that, things could get really hairy.

A woman scorned was one thing. But a female reporter scorned was something entirely different.

He tried to remain cordial and keep things on an impersonal level, but Gretchen wasn't making things easy.

"I have no qualms about moving a couple of name tags," she said, with a cherry-red smile.

"That sounds appealing, but it's my job to rub elbows with some of the vintners this evening." Sullivan scanned the mingling crowd, looking for Lissa. He could use a little help slipping away from Gretchen.

Several times during the past half hour, he'd searched the room and caught Lissa's eye, only to have his gaze ricochet off an unreadable expression.

Was she mad about something? Did she think he'd dropped the ball because he'd been lusting after the busty reporter who'd tried to attach herself to his hip?

Lissa needed to understand this thing with Gretchen wasn't going anywhere, that as attractive— and obviously willing—as Gretchen was, Sullivan wouldn't let things take a sexual and unprofessional turn.

"Excuse me," Ken Cartwright said, addressing his guests. "May I have your attention?"

Ah, a way out. Thank goodness.

People gradually grew silent and turned toward their host, allowing Ken to continue his speech. "My daughter Lissa has worked with me for years, learning everything I know about wine. And I think she's surpassed anything I've ever done.''

The guests smiled and looked at Lissa, then at her father.

''My daughter has created a new blend called Virgin Mist,'' Ken said, pride evident in every word. ''And we'd like you to try a glass before we officially unveil it later this month.''

As the catering staff carried in silver platters laden with glasses, offering Virgin Mist to each guest, Sullivan couldn't help but study Lissa. She worried her bottom lip, undoubtedly waiting for the reaction of her peers, waiting for their response.

Sullivan should be at her side. It was his job to support her.

As glasses raised, a few murmurs rippled through the room. Anticipation grew steadily.

Taking the chance to untangle himself from the determined blonde, he said, ''It's been great talking to you, but it looks as though I'm back on the clock. Will you please excuse me?''

The woman gave him a sad-eyed pout, which he quickly dismissed. Leaving Gretchen, he made his way toward Lissa, but before he could reach her side, an older man eased close to her. It was the guy he'd seen her talking to earlier, although both seemed friendlier now.

The man was expensively dressed and the picture of refined charm. Handsome.

And he was also old enough to be her dad.

He whispered something that lit up her eyes. Complimenting her wine, Sullivan realized, as the other guests burst into nods and smiles.

Lissa appeared to be pleased with the attention. But Sullivan spotted masculine interest in the man's gaze, in his stance.

Ever since his ex had dumped him for a rich guy who was old enough for Medicare—or so Sullivan thought—those May-December things stuck in his craw.

What attracted a young woman to an old duck like that?

He'd always suspected Kristin had gone for Atwater's bucks. Not that Sullivan hadn't had money when they'd first married. He'd had a ton of it—all tied up in a trust fund, which his father had refused to release until after Sullivan had earned his first million.

And Kristin, apparently, had gotten tired of waiting.

Yet Lissa didn't seem to be the kind of woman who was attracted to a hefty bank account.

Maybe it was the father-thing, her being adopted and all. But even that psychological stretch didn't help Sullivan understand. Or make it any easier to accept.

The older gentleman intimated something to Lissa, and she laughed. Sullivan supposed the friendly exchange shouldn't bother him. The guy was probably one of the vintners in this region. A successful man, no doubt.

But as the evening unfolded, he learned a little more about the man who'd set his sights on Lissa.

Martinelli's second wife had died in a skiing accident last year, while vacationing with friends in Canada. The woman had also been fifteen years younger than Martinelli.

Why didn't the guy go after women his own age?

Not that Sullivan had staked any kind of claim on Lissa. Nor did he intend to. But there were plenty of guys in their thirties who would appreciate her, who were better suited.

Sullivan decided Anthony Martinelli was too old, too charming, too…too wrong for Lissa.

Much later, after the last guest had said goodbye at the door and Ken and Donna had disappeared upstairs, Lissa joined Sullivan near the fireplace. "So? What do you think?"

He thought that Gramps was making a play for her, but he knew that wasn't what she meant. "Everything went exceptionally well. Word will spread about Virgin Mist. And when we have the official unveiling later this month, Valencia Vineyards should become a force to be reckoned with in the wine industry."

A slow smile lit up her face, warming the emerald flecks in her eyes to a brilliant gleam. "Anthony said the same thing."

So, Sullivan had been right. The old guy had charmed her.

Normally, Sullivan didn't involve himself in his clients' personal affairs, but he couldn't help commenting this time. "Martinelli was making the moves on you all evening. And you're young enough to be his daughter."

She bristled.

Okay, maybe he shouldn't have said anything. But it was too late to backpedal now.

"Anthony was the epitome of grace and charm this evening," she said. "But on the other hand, that buxom reporter kept thrusting her chest at you and making a scene."

"I admit, Gretchen was pretty brazen. But I didn't take her up on her offer."

"She offered you sex?"

"Not with words." Sullivan crossed his arms, unsure of how or why they'd gotten into this conversation. But for some reason, he couldn't back off, couldn't keep that old baggage from surfacing. "But, in case you didn't notice, ol' Dapper Dad had the same idea. He just had more class and style."

Lissa blew out a heavy sigh. "You're crazy."

Maybe he was. But like a bulldog with his jaws locked on a meaty bone, Sullivan couldn't seem to let it go, let it drop. "Are you interested in him?"

Her brow furrowed, as though his question offended her. But she seemed to recover. "I might be interested. Anthony is a nice man."

"And he's old enough to be your father."

"So what?" She crossed her arms. A spark of anger brought a fire to her eyes. "Lots of women like older men."

"That's because they're either after money or a father figure."

"I'm not after anything."

Sullivan realized he should have kept his opinions to himself and wished he'd never brought up the subject. "I'm sorry. This really is none of my business. And the conversation is way out of line."

"You're right."

"Forgive me?" Sullivan asked, tossing her a playful grin meant to appease her.

She paused for a moment, as though giving it some thought. "Apology accepted," she said. "It's been a long and stressful night. Maybe we should start fresh in the morning."

"Good idea." Sullivan placed a hand on her shoulder, felt the tension ease. "I won't say anything else about your choice of men."

"Thank you."

"I'll see you in the office at nine," Sullivan said, before turning and heading out the door.

Lissa watched him go. The words they'd spoken still hung in the air.

Lots of women like older guys.

They're either after money or a father figure.

Money had never been important to her. Not so important that she'd be attracted to a man's financial portfolio. So there went the first of Sullivan's theories.

And she had a wonderful father, a man who'd been good to her, even if he wasn't her *real* father. And that took care of Sullivan's other older man/younger woman theory.

Besides having a lot in common, she found Anthony attractive and his attention flattering.

Yet another explanation rose to the forefront.

Anthony was the first man who'd taken an interest in her, and that had to count for something.

No, the "father thing" had nothing to do with it.

Chapter Five

Jared slowed his black Lexus at the fork in the road then followed the route he'd mapped to Valencia Vineyards. The damaged files from the Children's Connection had raised a lot of questions, and he hoped this two-hour trek from Portland would provide some answers.

From the bits and pieces of charred paper the private investigator had painstakingly studied and put together, Jared learned that Olivia had given birth to a boy named Adam Bartlite. And apparently, Adam had grown up on a vineyard. At least, that's the address his adoptive parents had given the clinic.

A search of county land records revealed that Ken and Donna Cartwright had owned the property for nearly forty years. For that reason, Jared suspected that Adam's father was probably the caretaker or another employee who was provided with family lodging on the property.

After proceeding a mile down the road, a big Ponderosa-style sign told Jared he'd found the place. He turned in and followed a long, winding drive past rows upon rows of grapevines growing on the rolling hillsides.

He assumed Adam had grown up on the vineyard, although there was a good chance the young man no longer lived here. His parents could have retired or moved on. Or he might have gone off to college and settled into a career near his alma mater, as Jared had done. But surely someone at the vineyard would remember the Bartlites, even if the family had moved away.

Jared wasn't sure how his firstborn would take the surprise appearance of his biological father, but they'd have to deal with that when the time came. The first step was locating the boy—or rather the man.

As he pulled up to the house, a large, wood-and-glass structure with an A-framed entry, Jared parked and climbed from the car. His pulse raced with anticipation as he approached the front door.

At seventeen, Jared hadn't been ready to take on the responsibility of being a father, nor had he wanted to marry a teenage girl he barely knew. But now that he'd matured and had a family of his own, he felt as though he'd let the kid down, even if Adam had been raised in a happy home.

Jared would like to make amends—somehow. Not that he had any legal responsibility; but morally, he did.

He knocked on the door. When no one answered right away, he rang the bell.

When was the last time he'd felt so nervous? He couldn't remember.

A petite older woman with strawberry-blond hair answered the door.

"Mrs. Cartwright?" he asked.

"Yes."

"I'm Jared Cambry. And I'm looking for Adam Bartlite."

She furrowed her brow. "I'm afraid I don't know anyone by that name."

A dead end?

Sam Hastings, the private investigator, had photocopied the charred scraps of paper, all that remained of a file on Olivia Maddison. Had this address been part of another adoption case? He supposed it was possible.

"There was a fire at the Children's Connection clinic that destroyed many of their records, so my information is sketchy at best. But this is the address that was in the file." Jared tugged at the knot in his tie.

The woman straightened and tucked a strand of hair behind her ear. "We adopted our daughter from the

Children's Connection. But we don't know anyone by the name of Bartlite.''

Maybe Adam and his parents had only lived here a short while and she'd forgotten.

''My son would be twenty-seven years old,'' Jared said, trying to jar the woman's memory, hoping he hadn't hit an insurmountable wall.

''Our Lissa is twenty-seven.''

A coincidence? Or merely a mix-up of the scanty records they'd pieced together?

Grasping for a straw, Jared asked, ''Do you know anything about her birth parents?''

''Not much. Just a few details. But that's because an old high-school friend of mine worked at Portland General for a while. I was curious, so she gave me a bit of information.''

''What did you learn?''

''Lissa's mother was only seventeen. She'd intended to keep her baby, but was involved in a car accident that left her in a coma. The doctors delivered Lissa prematurely, and the poor mother died shortly after the birth.''

Hope jumpstarted Jared's pulse. ''Was the mother's name Olivia Maddison?''

Mrs. Cartwright sobered, furrowed a delicate brow and held on to the doorjamb. ''Lissa's mother's name was Olivia. But that's all I know. What's all this about?''

''I think I may be Lissa's biological father.'' The revelation made him feel grossly inadequate. Why hadn't he come looking for his child sooner? Come before a crisis made him look as if he would have stayed anonymous forever.

"But you were looking for Adam Bartlite," she said, as though trying to negate his tie to her daughter.

"I'm not sure where or how Adam Bartlite fits into the picture. Maybe he was a child whose records had been mixed with Lissa's when the clinic staff tried to salvage what they could."

It really didn't matter. Not anymore. He'd found what he was looking for—his child. A daughter.

Mrs. Cartwright pursed her lips and looked at him as if he were the angel of death. "What do you want from us?"

"Nothing," he lied, not ready to reveal his purpose. "I just want to meet her, maybe get to know her."

The woman who'd nurtured his child studied him critically. Assessing his character, he supposed. And maybe trying to spot a telltale resemblance. When she caught his gaze, her mouth parted. "Your eyes are the same shade as hers."

"Was she born on January the thirteenth at Portland General Hospital?"

The woman nodded, but didn't speak. She didn't have to.

Jared tried to keep the excitement—and hope—from his voice. "Is she here?"

"She's down at the vineyard office."

Apprehension slammed into him. And so did shame. He should have looked for her sooner.

What if she wasn't happy to see him? What if she thought he was using her? In a sense, he was. Questions bombarded him. But the biggest one rang loud and clear. What if Lissa didn't care about the life-or-death situation facing her biological father's family?

"How do you think she'll feel about me showing up unannounced?" he asked, hoping the child he'd given up wouldn't harbor any ill feelings.

"I'm not sure."

"Maybe she'll resent me for not being a part of her life," Jared said, revealing his fears. "Resent me for giving her up."

"Lissa is a lovely young woman. And there's not a day goes by that I don't thank the Good Lord for giving her to us. I'd been unable to get pregnant for years, and I'd wanted a baby desperately." Tears welled in her eyes, and she tried to blink them back.

"I don't want to interfere in her life or take her away from you. I'd just like to get to know her."

Mrs. Cartwright nodded. "I can't blame you for that. It might have been more difficult for me had you come looking for her while she was still a child."

Jared tried to put himself in Mrs. Cartwright's shoes. If someone showed up on his doorstep wanting to lay claim to one of his kids, he'd be concerned, too. "Thank you for loving her, for being her mother."

"It's been a joy and an honor, Mr. Cambry." Then

she grabbed a sweater from a coat rack in the hall. "Come along with me. I'll introduce you. The rest is up to Lissa."

She had that right.

How would Lissa react when she met him? And more important, what would she say when he asked her to be tested as a bone-marrow donor?

He would find out soon enough.

Lissa bent over the desk where Sullivan had displayed a marketing plan he'd developed. She might have put away any romantic ideas involving the handsome consultant, but she couldn't overlook his musky, mountain-meadow scent, couldn't ignore the brush of his arm against hers, the heat that raced through her blood. Nor could she keep her eyes off him.

He'd dressed casually today in jeans and a white dress shirt. Rolled sleeves revealed muscular forearms and an expensive gold watch.

"So, what do you think?" he asked.

Okay. Mind back on business. "As I've already mentioned, I think your idea of opening the vineyard and winery for tours is a good one. I'll discuss it with my father when he gets back from San Diego."

Sullivan nodded, as a light rap sounded at the office door. Before Lissa could answer, her mother turned the knob and let herself in. A tall, dark-haired stranger followed her.

"Honey," her mom began. "I know you're busy, but there's someone I think you should meet."

Lissa straightened and approached her mother and the middle-aged man. His eyes seemed to study her with more curiosity than was the norm. Who was he?

"I'm Jared Cambry." The man extended a hand in greeting, his green eyes scanning her face, her expression.

His name didn't sound familiar, but Lissa shook his hand. "Lissa Cartwright."

"You look like your mother," he said.

Lissa glanced at Donna and wrinkled her brow. Eileen was the one who favored their mother. Was the guy blind?

"He means Olivia," Donna said, her voice soft. And a little wobbly.

Olivia was her birth mother's name. Did this guy know her real mother? Her real parents? A multitude of questions tumbled forth. But, for the life of her, the words wouldn't form.

"I have reason to believe I'm your father," the man said.

Lissa found it difficult to speak, to think. To react.

She finally said, "I'm a bit overwhelmed." But flabbergasted was more like it. As a little girl, she'd always envisioned her real parents coming for her, but they usually arrived in a coach like Cinderella's.

"I can understand your surprise," he said.

Could he? As a kid, she'd dreamed of this day. Lived for it. But now? She wasn't sure. Why had he come looking for her? To assuage his guilt? To satisfy his curiosity? Had he thought about her often? Prayed she was loved and cared for?

A childlike hope sprang from nowhere, wishing he'd say that he'd been searching for her for years, that he'd never meant to give her away.

"I'd been meaning to find you," he said, "ever since moving back to Portland last year. But I hadn't gotten around to it. I'm an attorney, and I've been trying to set up a new office. Now my family is faced with a crisis. And I'm hoping you can help."

Did he want money? She quickly scanned his length, taking in the expensive, gray three-piece suit, the pale yellow shirt. The classy tie.

He didn't appear to be poor or struggling.

"What kind of crisis?" she asked.

"My youngest son, your half brother, was diagnosed with a rare blood disorder. And he needs a bone-marrow transplant."

A myriad of emotions swirled in her heart. Surprise that he'd walked into her life. Curiosity, too. But it seemed as though he'd only come looking for her because he stood to lose something. Someone special to him.

He hadn't been looking for *her*.

"Mark is only eight years old." The man pulled a wallet from the inside pocket of his jacket, withdrew a photograph of a kid in a soccer uniform and handed it to her. "He's a bright and loving little boy—the greatest kid in the world. Without a transplant, he won't live to see his tenth birthday.''

She looked into the smiling face of a dark-haired child with a splatter of freckles across his nose and a bright-eyed grin.

Her brother?

Her *half* brother.

This was all so overwhelming. She needed time to think. To react.

As though wanting some direction, some guidance, she glanced at her mother. The poor thing looked as though she was about to fall apart.

Lissa's gaze drifted to Sullivan, who stood on the sidelines watching the scene unfold. She supposed it might have been better to meet privately with Mr. Cambry. But in a way, she welcomed the presence of others, appreciated their silent support. An audience made holding back the tears much easier.

''Whether you're a match or not, I'd still like to establish a relationship with you,'' Mr. Cambry…Jared said. For goodness' sake. What was she supposed to call him?

Torn in a hundred different pieces, Lissa again looked to her mother, as though Donna could save the day, as she'd always done in the past. But this was a decision Lissa would have to make on her own. At least the father-daughter-relationship stuff.

She wouldn't, of course, refuse to help his son. She glanced at the photo she held in her hand. The boy's name was Mark. And he was much too young to be facing death.

Jared scanned the small, woodsy office, as though noticing the others for the first time, then focused on Lissa. "I'm sorry for blurting out news I should have revealed in private. But I've been so eager to find you...."

Because of the boy, she realized. Not because of her.

"Maybe we could have an early lunch together and discuss this further?" he asked. "We can drive into the nearest town. I noticed several cafés and diners as I passed through."

"I'm afraid not," Lissa answered. "I'm much too busy to take a lunch break today. But I'll have the required testing done in the next day or so. Just let me know where I need to go. And if I'm a match, I'll donate bone marrow to your son."

Her brother.

"Thank you," Jared said. "I can't ask for more than that. But I really meant what I said about having a relationship with you—regardless of how everything else works out."

She nodded, but again her voice failed her. For some reason, she didn't want to make promises—or accept any—that might not pan out.

Her mother finally spoke. "I'll walk you back to your car, Mr. Cambry."

"All right." Jared withdrew a business card from his wallet, wrote down several phone numbers. Then handed it to Lissa. "Please call me. Anytime of the day or night."

Again she nodded, but when she returned the photo to him, he refused to take it. "Please keep it. I'd like you to have it."

Lissa stood like a concrete angel in the center of a cemetery until the door shut behind her mother and her father—or rather, the guy who'd provided half her genetic makeup.

And, in spite of a determination to keep her feelings locked inside where Sullivan would never see, the tears slipped down her face. She set the picture of the boy—Mark—on the desktop, then wiped her eyes and nibbled at her lip.

Oh, God. Don't let me fall apart here, in front of Sullivan. She could only imagine what the consultant was thinking of the surreal event that had just taken place.

Sullivan had been watching the awkward meeting, but only because he couldn't find a graceful way to leave the room. He'd never been a sucker for tears, but as Lissa's pain became evident, washing a path down her cheeks, it was tough to remain silent or invisible.

"Hey, if you'd like some time to sort through all of this, I understand. I can go for a walk." He nodded toward the doggie bed on the floor. "I can even take Barney."

"That's all right," she said, sniffling. "We've got a lot of work to do."

Yeah? If the situation were reversed, Sullivan would need time to regroup.

Did she expect to switch gears and keep going? Apparently so, because she stood over the desk and began to peruse the paperwork he'd already laid before her. But before they could return to the business discussion they'd been having, another wave of tears surfaced.

"I'm sorry." She sniffled and wiped her face with the back of a hand.

"It's none of my business," he said, "but it seems to me as though you don't want to talk to the guy. I'd think you'd be curious about your roots."

"I *am* curious. But what if I reach out to him, and then he disappears from my life when the tests show I'm not a match for his son?" She blew out a ragged sigh. "To tell you the truth, I'm afraid of getting close, then having him turn his back on me after he gets what he wants."

If anyone understood rejection—the fear of loving someone and having them walk out—it was Sullivan. Without a conscious thought, he slipped an arm around her and gave her a friendly squeeze. He didn't say anything, though. Hell, he didn't have any training in this kind of touchy-feely stuff.

But apparently, he'd lucked out. Lissa hadn't needed any words of wisdom, because she leaned into his embrace, drawing comfort he didn't usually offer anyone.

They stood there for a while, not talking, not really moving. But something weird began to happen. The friendly hug triggered a powerful awareness of Lissa as a woman.

She fit nicely in his arms. A little too nicely. Sullivan couldn't help savoring her scent—something that reminded him of a peach orchard in the spring. And he grew pleasantly aware of the softness of her breasts as they pressed against his chest.

Without a conscious effort, his hands slid along the contour of her back, offering comfort, while providing proof of the curves she hid behind loose-fitting clothes.

He had an unwelcome urge to brush a kiss against her hair, to nuzzle her cheek. But he refrained. And even though he meant to keep things between them on a business level, he continued to hold her, unwilling to let go until she'd had her full dose of compassion and pulled away.

Lissa could have remained in Sullivan's arms all day and into the night.

His musky scent taunted her. While he held her against his hard, muscular chest, she fought the urge not to nestle against him.

His hands slid up and down her back—in an effort to comfort her, no doubt. And she found her body stirring, her hormones begging for more than a friendly touch.

But there was too much going on in her life right now, too many emotions running amok. She didn't need to shoot herself in the foot by reading more into his embrace than he intended.

She took a deep breath, stepped out of his arms, then let the air go, deflating her lungs and her silly dreams. How could she make something out of his efforts to be kind and supportive?

"I'm sorry for falling apart in front of you." She offered a wobbly smile. "You're proving to be a friend, as well as a business associate."

He nodded. "Are you sure you don't want to take the guy up on the offer to talk?"

No. She wasn't sure about anything.

"We can discuss marketing later," Sullivan added. "Even if you don't want to see him, maybe you need to take a walk or something."

It wouldn't help. The questions that had been brewing for years, the questions she hadn't asked her father while he was here, would only prod her into doing what she needed to do.

She reached into her pocket and pulled out the business card he'd given her. She flipped it over and spotted the home and cell phone numbers he'd written on the back.

He couldn't have gotten far.

She placed a hand on Sullivan's cheek. "Thanks for understanding."

Then she picked up the telephone and placed a call to Jared Cambry's cell phone.

Lissa and Jared sat across from each other at the Golden Corkscrew, a trendy little restaurant that offered the best food and drink the Pacific Northwest had to offer.

For the most part, their plates remained untouched, a silent testimony that they had too much to talk about, too many reasons not to eat.

Lissa agreed to have her blood drawn at the Portland General annex lab located at the clinic in town, before heading back to the vineyard. And Jared promised to let her know as soon as he'd heard anything.

But their conversation didn't end there, and Lissa believed he might be telling her the truth, that he might actually want a relationship with her, whether she was able to donate bone marrow or not.

He'd shown her photos of his wife, Danielle—a pretty woman with curly brown hair that reached her shoulders. From the way he talked about the woman, Lissa suspected they had a loving marriage, just like her parents had.

She still had the photograph of Mark, the boy who needed a bone-marrow donor. And through wallet-sized pictures, she met her other two siblings—seventeen-year-old Chad, who wore a football uniform and held his helmet, and fifteen-year-old Shawna, a pretty girl with braces.

"That's an older picture of Shawna," Jared said. "She's had her braces off for about six months."

"I'd like to meet them," Lissa said. "Someday. I'm pretty busy right now, with the launching of the blend."

Jared smiled warmly. "Your parents must be very proud of you. I certainly am. And I'd like to order a case of Virgin Mist as soon as it goes on sale."

She returned his smile, glad that he'd recognized her accomplishment and wanted to be supportive. "It'll be on the market after the reception later this month."

"Well, I hope the unveiling is everything you want it to be and more."

"Thanks. It will be a pretty special event. And I'll probably have to break down and go shopping." She blew out a sigh. "I hate dressing up."

"Why?" he asked. "Most women love that stuff."

"Dressing up just draws attention to me and makes me feel awkward."

"I don't know why. You're a beautiful woman, Lissa."

Her mother had said as much on many occasions. Her dad, too. But for some reason, hearing Jared compliment her made it almost seem true.

"I've got a ton of self-confidence when it comes to the vineyard, to farming and making wine, but…" She let the words drop.

Jared reached across the table and took her hand. "You and I are going shopping. I'm going to buy you a whole new wardrobe, one that makes you feel good enough to stand out in a crowd.''

"Oh, no," she said. "You don't need to do that."

"But I want to. It's a very small way to make up for not being there for you." He gave her hand a squeeze. "Please? It'll be fun."

She didn't know about fun. But it might be interesting to go shopping with the man. Her dad never liked that sort of thing, leaving all the household and family purchases to her mother.

Jared motioned for the waitress and asked for their check. "I'm going to spring for a whole makeover, starting at that hair salon down the street."

The salon? Lissa lifted her hand and fingered the heavy bun resting on top of her head. She hadn't had a trim in ages. Of course, she'd never agree to a full-on haircut unless a personal beautician or a step-by-step styling lesson came with it.

"You're a lovely woman, Lissa. And it's only right that you let an expert enhance your basic beauty."

Was he right? Did she have something a stylist could work with?

Jared's excitement and sincerity were hard to ignore. What would her mother say when she returned home in a new outfit and a different hairstyle—one she could handle on her own.

Or better yet, what would Sullivan say?

Would it make a difference? Would he find her attractive? Someone he wouldn't mind taking to bed?

"All right," she said, her attraction to Sullivan influencing the crazy decision.

"Great. Let's get started."

The first stop was a dress shop, where Jared took an active part in choosing a new wardrobe, one with bright colors that set off her green eyes and showed off more of her body than she'd otherwise been comfortable revealing.

The last purchase was a green silky top that hugged her waist and a formfitting black skirt.

"Can she wear that out of the store?" Jared asked.

"Certainly," the happy sales clerk said. "I'll cut off the tags."

"Thank you for doing this," Lissa said. "It's been kind of fun, actually."

"My pleasure," he said. "I've enjoyed watching you blossom. Now let's go to the salon."

Lissa glanced at her watch. It was getting late. And she probably should head back to the office, where Sullivan would be waiting for her. "That's not necessary."

"Indulge me," Jared said, green eyes shimmering.

Oh, what the heck. "All right."

Two hours later, Lissa sat before a mirror in the beauty salon, unable to believe the change in her. Of course, she'd sometimes had two people working on her at a time, but she'd managed to squeeze in a manicure and a pedicure.

Antoine, the male stylist, had used a henna rinse to bring out the natural color of her hair. He trimmed the ends and talked her into some layering that created a full, flowing effect, insisting that one of her most attractive features, other than the big green eyes, was her waist-length hair.

The talented stylist had created a miracle, leaving Lissa with a sensual look she'd never expected.

"You can still twist it and braid it," Antoine said, "but wear it loose whenever you want to make an impression on people, particularly men."

Do you ever let your hair down? Sullivan had once asked her.

A burst of confidence bubbled forth. What would he say, when she returned to the vineyard? Would he be pleased? Aroused?

And if so, then what?

Would she have the courage to flirt? To actually offer herself to him?

She turned her head, watching the strands flow gracefully down her back like a long, silky veil.

Funny, but she didn't feel vulnerable or exposed now. Not at all.

"Renee," Antoine called the makeup artist who'd been waiting nearby. "We're ready to add the finishing touch."

When Renee finished instructing her in the art of makeup application, as well as adding lipstick, blush and mascara, Lissa couldn't believe her eyes.

She looked like a new woman.

Heck, she even felt like a new woman.

A beautiful woman.

Lissa couldn't wait to see the look on Sullivan's face when she knocked upon the cottage door and asked if he'd like to share a glass of wine and watch the sunset.

And if he appeared impressed?

Who knew what else she might ask him to share?

Chapter Six

Before climbing from her silver Honda Prelude, Lissa couldn't help but take one last look at her reflection in the rearview mirror.

For the first time in her life, she saw a stylish woman gazing back at her. The light application of sage-colored shadow and dark-brown mascara highlighted the green of her eyes. And a feathered layering of the hair at the side of her face softened the plain, yet harsh style she'd worn before.

Jared had been right.

The makeover had done wonders for her appearance. And it raised her confidence level to an all-time high.

She slid from the car, then tugged at the short,

black skirt, making sure it hadn't hiked up, revealing a pair of thong panties the sales lady insisted all the young women were wearing.

"I don't want Shawna ever learning I bought you those," Jared had said with a smile. "She's growing up too fast as it is."

Well, it seemed as though Lissa had grown up overnight. Or rather, during the course of an afternoon in town with her biological father.

They'd driven to Valley View Clinic, which housed an annex lab of Portland General Hospital. A technician drew the necessary blood for the preliminary testing, and Lissa signed a form allowing the results to be divulged to Jared.

After giving Jared a hug, Lissa promised to come to Portland soon. Meeting with him had answered a lot of her questions about her origin and her feelings of abandonment.

Jared hadn't been ready to marry a girl he hardly knew, a teen who refused his calls. And although he'd wanted to provide for Olivia and her baby, Olivia had shut him out.

It was anyone's guess what would have happened had Lissa's birth mother lived.

But one thing was certain. Lissa's life would have been dramatically different from the one that she knew. And to be perfectly honest, she couldn't imagine not having Ken and Donna Cartwright as parents. Or Eileen as a sister.

In many ways, Jared still seemed like a stranger,

but she sensed they could become friends. Or maybe something more—given time.

Once in her car, she picked up the cell phone and called home.

"I was so worried," her mother said. "Mr. Cambry looked like a decent sort, but you never know."

"Actually, he was very nice, Mom."

"Will you be seeing him again?"

"I may drive into Portland and meet his family later in the month, but I have too much going on even to consider it until after the reception next week."

"I'm making a pot roast for dinner," her mom said. "Your favorite. If you see Sullivan, tell him I'm setting an extra plate."

"Will do. I'm going straight to the office when I get back, since Sullivan and I still have a lot to get done today."

"You work so hard, honey. I wish you would take more time for yourself."

Lissa planned to take her mom's advice as soon as she got back to the vineyard, if everything worked out. Because even though she and Sullivan had a lot to discuss, her first order of business was gauging his reaction to the new Lissa.

When she arrived at the vineyard office, she found Sullivan and Barney gone, so she headed to the cottage, where she assumed he and the puppy would be. As she strode across the small suspension bridge in a brand new pair of high heels, she realized even her walk had changed since the afternoon makeover.

Had she acquired a swivel-hipped swagger like

Gretchen's? Amazing. And she didn't feel the least bit klutzy.

Yet, as she approached the deck in front of his house, a brief wave of nervousness swept through her tummy. But she managed to get a grip on it.

For goodness' sake, it's not like she was going to seduce the man. All she really needed to do was get an idea of how he might react to the idea of making love to her. She could always broach the subject another day.

Or change her mind completely.

This was merely a little sexual experimentation. She certainly didn't intend to pounce on Sullivan before dinner.

She'd probably start by asking about Barney. Then she'd thank him for encouraging her to meet with Jared. And if that went well, maybe she'd suggest a glass of wine on the porch.

Of course, she wasn't sure how far she'd go with a sexual proposition. She'd have to play that by ear. Asking a man to be her one-time lover might be awkward, but she was determined not to be a virgin the rest of her life.

And that meant taking control of her destiny, even if she took a tumble. What was that they said about falling from the horse? Well, she'd just climb right back on.

With her new confidence riding high in the saddle, Lissa rapped soundly upon the door.

Cowgirl up.

Moments later, Sullivan answered, wearing a pair

of faded jeans and a white T-shirt. Gorgeous, as usual. But it wasn't his casual, playboy stance that tickled her arousal. It was the expression on his face.

"Lissa." His eyes widened and his jaw dropped. "I…uh…wow."

She'd caused him to stutter. Imagine that. And it was a good kind of stutter. His eyes swept over her, and, without a doubt, she knew he liked what he saw.

His reaction was empowering.

Lissa had never evoked that kind of wide-eyed effect on anyone, let alone a man she found so darn attractive. Her confidence soared, and she felt like singing "Yippee-Ki-Yay." But there was no reason to let him think she'd had a makeover with him in mind.

"I went shopping for an outfit to wear to the reception and decided to have my hair done while I was in town. Since Virgin Mist is so much a part of me, I thought we both needed a fresh package. Do you like my new look?"

"Like it? It's great. *You* look great." He raked a hand through his hair, then seemed to regroup. He opened the door and stepped aside. "Come on in."

Before she could ask about Barney, she spotted the pup curled up on the sofa, chewing on one of Sullivan's socks.

"Thanks for babysitting."

"No problem," he said, his eyes still scanning her from head to toe and back again. The heated gaze caressed her, causing her heart to flutter, her blood to warm, her courage to soar.

She placed a hand on her hip, feeling the sleek green fabric that outlined her shape. "I'm glad you suggested I talk to Jared. It did me a lot of good."

"I can see that," he said, his eyes following her hand movement. "It must have been one hell of a conversation."

It was working. She'd caught his interest. So why not push the envelope a little further? "How about a glass of wine before dinner?"

"Yeah. Sure." Sullivan went to the kitchenette, pulled a bottle of wine from the fridge, then fumbled through the drawers, looking for a corkscrew.

Was he nervous?

Because of her?

That was encouraging—to say the least.

"Let me," she said, entering the small, confined area. The dinky kitchen was barely large enough for one, let alone two. But she liked the idea of rubbing elbows with Sullivan, of bumping him with her hip, brushing her shoulder against his upper arm.

He must have liked it, too, because he just stood there with a mesmerized look on his face.

Merely inches apart, neither of them moved. Their gazes locked, and she could almost hear his heartbeat, feel him breathing. He reached out and took a lock of her hair in his hand, fingering the silky strands. "I'd wanted to see it loose like this."

As her hair slid through his fingers, his eyes darkened, and his expression sobered.

Lissa had read about that kind of heated reaction in romance novels and had seen it on the big screen at the movie-theater in town. But she'd never experienced it firsthand.

A woman could sure get used to seeing desire brewing in a man's eyes, to seeing the hunger. Especially if that desire and hunger were for her.

According to the books she'd read and the movies she'd seen, Sullivan should take her in his arms and kiss her about now.

Was he thinking about it?

Or did he need a cue?

Lissa didn't want to be part of the audience any longer. Nor did she want to let life—or rather a once-in-a-lifetime opportunity—pass her by. She placed a hand upon his jaw, brushed a thumb across the faint bristle of his cheek, felt her body coming alive.

He did nothing to stop her, nothing to let her know she'd overstepped her boundaries. So she slid her hand to the back of his neck and drew his lips to hers.

And just as she'd seen lovers do on the silver screen, she closed her eyes, waiting for the world to spin out of control.

And boy howdy, did it spin.

Sullivan had no idea where his business ethics had run off to, but when Lissa pulled his mouth to hers, he'd nearly come unglued at the seams.

This was crazy. Foolish. But he couldn't seem to stop the kiss. Nor could he keep from dipping his tongue into her willing mouth, exploring the wet, velvety softness that opened for him.

Her hair flowed around them like a sensual veil.

And desire shot right through him. He pulled her flush against a demanding erection and caressed her back. But that wasn't enough. He wanted to touch more of her, to experience all she had to offer.

His hands sought her breasts, and all the while, his tongue explored her mouth.

Had any other woman tasted so sweet?

Just hours ago, he'd found her interesting. Admirable. But how in the world had this beautiful, sexy woman mystically evolved from a mild-mannered, levelheaded businesswoman?

Ah, man. Business.

What had Lissa done to him? And where was his body taking his mind?

With reluctance, his hand withdrew from the fullness of her breast, and he ended the kiss, trying to break the spell that had clouded his mind and turned him inside out. "I…uh…don't know what got into me. I make it a point not to mix business with pleasure."

"What can I do to change your mind?" she asked, her voice husky. A red flush on her neck and chest told him the startling kiss had aroused her, too.

"I shouldn't change my mind," he said. *Shouldn't*. But he sure as hell wanted to.

The minute she'd entered the guest house, he'd lost sight of anything but the stunning woman who'd made a swanlike transformation. The change had unbalanced him, and he struggled with fascination, with attraction—not to mention a mind-boggling case of lust.

"I realize a full-blown affair might make things sticky," she said. "But what about a one-time fling? If we kept it a secret between the two of us, no one would ever need to know."

She was asking him to make love to her?

The suggestion both startled and aroused him. He probably ought to decline, but for some reason, the words didn't form.

As her fingers fiddled with the top button of her blouse, he found it even more difficult to speak.

Her hands dropped to the next button, and he realized she was undressing. Or was she just teasing him?

Two buttons undone.

She took it slowly, as if it was her first time taking off her clothes in front of a man. The act of innocence taunted him, tempting him to distraction. But she knew exactly what she was doing, had probably done it many times before. And it was working on him. Big time.

Hell, he'd been so busy these past couple of months that he couldn't remember the last time he'd had sex. Maybe that's what had gotten into him, pumping his blood, making his hormones take control of his body.

Three buttons.

Her slow, sensuous efforts revealed a black satiny bra.

Sullivan liked the feel of satin, liked the look of black underwear on fair skin. But he also liked to avoid commitment-bound women looking for a husband.

Of course, Lissa was a career-minded woman, not a nester. And right now, she was behaving more like a player.

Four.

Only two more to go. She wasn't going to stop, was she?

"Lady, you're driving me crazy. And making it difficult to keep my mind on business."

A smile tickled her lips, revealing that she knew exactly what she was doing to him. And that she was well aware of the blood-pounding effect it was having on him.

Put a stop to this, his conscience demanded. But a rebellious erection refused to listen.

As the last two buttons bit the dust, Sullivan sucked in a breath. What he wouldn't give to reach inside her open blouse, touch her skin, tease her the same way she was toying with him. But she'd set a strip-tease in motion, and for the life of him, he couldn't stop the show.

She slid the green, slinky material off her shoulders and let it slip to the kitchen floor. Next came the formfitting skirt. She unzipped it at the side, then pushed it down her hips. When it dropped to the linoleum, she kicked it aside.

Her hair hung over her shoulders and to her waist, but it couldn't hide the black bra and...oh, wow...a skimpy pair of black thong panties.

And to think, she'd been hiding that beautiful figure behind dull, baggy clothing—which was a real shame, as far as he was concerned.

As she silently offered her body, he sensed a slight hesitation, a gaze seeking his permission. Her sensual act of innocence enflamed his libido.

"Ah, Lissa." Her name slipped out of his mouth in near reverence.

She unhooked her bra and let it slide away, revealing two near-perfect breasts with taut nipples begging to be touched, stroked, kissed. And as she removed the little black panties, he was lost in a swirl of heat and desire.

"You don't make it easy for a guy to be ethical," he said, entranced by her beauty, by the gift of her body.

Like Lady Godiva, she stood before him, awaiting his acceptance with springtime-green eyes that promised renewal and awakening.

"I want you to make love to me, Sullivan."

Unable to fight the blood-pounding arousal any longer, he took her in his arms and claimed her mouth as his own. The kiss deepened, with tongues mating, hands seeking. Passion ignited and burned out of control.

A groan sounded low in his throat, as he tried to remove his clothes without taking his mouth from hers, without removing his hands from her silky skin, from her beaded nipples, her full breasts.

Finally, he had to pull away, his breath coming out in pants. "Did you bring any protection?"

Her jaw dropped, and her eyes widened. "You don't have any?"

"I came here for business purposes," he said, hoping and praying he still had a spare condom in his shaving kit. He'd thought about tossing it out ages ago, but for some reason, had left it there. For an emergency like this, he supposed.

He took her hand and led her into the bathroom. As he fumbled in the black leather bag, his fingers struck pay dirt, and he let out a sigh. "We're in luck."

Then he withdrew the worn foil-wrapped treasure, and took her to his bed.

He supposed there was time to back out, to change his mind. But better judgment be damned. He'd deal with the repercussions later.

After quickly shedding his clothes and shielding himself with the condom, he urged her onto the bed, then quickly made up for lost time. His hands slid along her silky skin, appreciating each gentle, womanly curve. He kissed her throat, her chest, her belly.

He ought to take it slow, savor her taste. But he was ready to explode. And if he didn't bury himself deep within her soon, he'd die from want of her.

Passion brewed in those big green eyes, begging him to love her thoroughly. Had it been that long for her, too?

He hovered over her. "Are you sure about this?"

She nodded. "More sure than you'll ever know. I want to feel you inside of me."

And that's just where he wanted to be. But as he entered her, she caught her breath.

Was she a virgin? She must be. She was so tight, ready but unyielding.

Damn it. And she hadn't told him, warned him. He started to pull back, to withdraw.

"Don't stop," she said, holding him close. "Don't you dare stop."

"It's your first time," he said. "And it's going to hurt."

"I don't care." She tilted her hips, making her needs and desires known.

Sullivan didn't think there was a man alive who could have reined in his passion and heeded his conscience at a time like this, so he thrust forward, breaking any resistance and completing the act she'd set into motion.

So tight, so willing.

He increased the tempo, and she arched up to receive each of his thrusts until he reached a mind-spinning, body-trembling climax. When the last wave of pleasure had passed, he continued to hold her, afraid to face the moment of truth.

In a way, he felt honored, as though he'd been given a gift he didn't deserve. But he also felt trapped.

He'd never made love to a virgin before. Wasn't there some kind of responsibility or obligation a woman's first lover was supposed to assume?

Sullivan didn't have a clue, although he felt some kind of moral responsibility that put a guilt trip on him.

And to make matters worse, he'd always prided himself in knowing the lady in his arms had enjoyed lovemaking as much as he had. There was no way it had been good for her, so in effect, he felt like a failure.

He was drowning in guilt and remorse. Fear, too.

Because he wasn't sure what she'd expect from him now.

As Sullivan rolled to the side, taking Lissa with him, she was caught up in a whirl of feelings she hadn't anticipated.

Making love had been better than she'd expected. Yes, there'd been pain. But there'd also been a rush, a feeling of power, of entering the realm of womanhood. And she'd experienced heat and desire, things she'd only read about before.

And once wouldn't be enough—especially with Sullivan working so closely with her for the next few weeks.

"Why didn't you tell me you were a virgin?" he asked.

Had she not measured up? Had he found her less desirable? "Would my virginity have made a difference?"

"I would have been more careful." He placed a hand on her hip, caressed it softly. "Are you okay?"

"I'm fine." She offered him a smile meant to absolve him from guilt. "It really didn't hurt much. And it should feel better next time."

"Next time?" he asked, his expression growing serious. "I thought this was a one-shot deal."

"Of course," she said, trying hard not to show her disappointment. "But *I* intend to have a next time."

He didn't answer.

Okay, so she desperately wanted to make love again. *With him.* But she'd only asked for a one-time fling, and she needed to let him off the hook.

She swallowed her disappointment and tried to save face. "I don't expect this to affect our business relationship."

"I won't let it," he said.

"Good." Then she rolled away from him and climbed out of bed.

"Where are you going?" he asked, still lying amidst rumpled sheets.

"To freshen up. Mom's having pot roast for dinner. And she's setting a place for you." She tossed a strand of hair over her shoulder, then went to retrieve her clothes from the kitchen.

She hoped her carefree departure left him with the idea that their lovemaking hadn't fazed her in the least. God forbid he got the idea that it had turned her life upside down. Or that he suspected she'd wanted to stay in bed with him until tomorrow morning. And maybe the next.

Or that he knew how badly she'd wanted him to ask her not to leave yet.

She freshened up in the bathroom and tried to put herself back together so her mother wouldn't suspect what they'd done, wouldn't lecture or—worse yet—start thinking about another wedding in the family.

A quick glance in the mirror revealed a red rash on her cheek, where his beard had chafed her. Great.

Well, there wasn't much she could do about that. Maybe her mom wouldn't notice.

Lissa conjured a light-hearted expression before leaving the bathroom. She found Sullivan sitting in the living room. He hadn't put on his clothes. She supposed they no longer had any reason to be modest.

"I wish it had been better for you," he said. "But for the record, it was good for me."

She offered him a smile. "I'm glad. And believe it or not, it was good for me, too."

"Tell your mother I'll be up as soon as I shower and change."

Lissa nodded, then picked up Barney from behind the recliner and walked out the front door.

Originally, she'd hoped to lose her virginity. Nothing more. Nothing less. But now she realized there was more to her game plan.

Making love to Sullivan had merely been the first step. Reaching an orgasm would be the next. But she couldn't imagine experiencing that with anyone other than Sullivan.

And she wondered what he'd do if she went back on her word and tried to seduce him again.

Chapter Seven

From the moment she and Sullivan entered the main house for dinner, Lissa acted as though nothing had happened between them. And Sullivan followed her lead.

It hadn't been an easy pretense, especially when her mother nearly dropped a bowl of mashed potatoes onto the carpet when Lissa walked into the dining room.

Mom stood near the table, the china bowl now clenched safely against her chest. "Oh my goodness, honey. You mentioned getting your hair done and buying a new dress, but you've...you've...blossomed."

"I thought that the wine and I could both use a

fresh new look.'' Lissa offered her mother a smile. It took all she had not to glance at Sullivan and check out his expression.

Was she afraid of what she might see? Or of what she might reveal?

Their lovemaking had touched her on a very personal level, making her complete. Making her feel like a desirable woman.

Had it been a positive experience for him, too?

''I can't get over it,'' her mom said, turning to Sullivan. ''Lissa is absolutely beautiful. Don't you agree?''

So much for avoiding eye contact with the man who'd sent her senses reeling, who'd helped her touch the moon and reach the stars.

Maybe it was her imagination but, for a moment, she thought she saw a glimmer of emotion in his eyes. But it quickly disappeared, as if it hadn't been there at all.

''She looks great,'' Sullivan said, sincerity in his gaze and truth in his tone. But not a hint of anything more.

It would have been nice to know what he was thinking or feeling, but he'd rolled back any evidence of his thoughts or emotions, tucking them way out of sight.

Well, what did she expect? She'd told him it would be their secret. And that she only wanted a one-time fling.

Hadn't he said he wouldn't allow their lovemaking

to interfere with business? And hadn't she agreed to do the same?

But Lissa hadn't realized how difficult that would be. She couldn't seem to get the smile-provoking memory of her first sexual encounter out of her mind.

The physical intimacy made her realize she wanted a man in her life, a lover. Not that the man had to be Sullivan, but that's who came to mind.

Could another lover replicate Sullivan's heated caresses and knee-buckling kisses?

She didn't think so.

And as much as she hated to admit it, her feelings had been affected by their lovemaking. In what way, she couldn't be sure.

Had Sullivan felt something, too? Something unexplainable?

She might never know, since she'd set the ball in motion by pretending they hadn't done anything special. But her course was set.

If they ever were to make love again, Sullivan would have to make the next move.

"Have a seat," her mother said, while placing the bowl of mashed potatoes onto the dining-room table. "I hope you like roast beef, Sullivan."

"I appreciate home-cooked meals, since I rarely get a chance to enjoy them." He took the seat across from Lissa. "And for the record, roast beef is one of my favorites."

Lissa wondered what other meals he liked. In spite

of their intimacy, there was a lot she didn't know about the man. A lot she'd like to find out.

Her mom returned to the table with a platter of meat and a bowl of vegetables. "Lissa, your dad called. He talked Uncle Pete into selling the house and moving to Oregon."

"Uncle Pete practically raised my father," Lissa said to Sullivan.

"There's a convalescent hospital not far from us," Mom added, while taking her seat and addressed Sullivan. "So we can be close enough to visit. Uncle Pete's wife died last summer. And since they'd never been blessed with children, he only has us."

"I think we need to bring him home to live here," Lissa said. "That way we can look after him."

"But what about his medical care?" Mom said.

"I'll be more than happy to help take care of him. And we can hire a nurse, if we need to. But I think Uncle Pete needs to spend the rest of his life with a family who loves him."

"I'm sure your father will agree," Mom said. "I'll talk to him about it after he gets home."

As Lissa passed the platter of beef to Sullivan, her mom clicked her tongue, slowly shook her head and grinned. "I can't get over the change in you."

Making love to Sullivan had been a stellar, life-changing event. Was the loss of her virginity as obvious as it felt?

Mom scrunched her eyes and cocked her head to

the side, her gaze still focused on Lissa. "What's that?"

"What's what?" Lissa picked up the bowl of gravy to hand to Sullivan.

"That red splotch on your face."

Oh, Lordy. Her mom had spotted the faint abrasion from the light stubble of Sullivan's afternoon shadow. Would she guess what they'd done this afternoon? Maybe insist upon having a little talk about sex being special and reserved for marriage?

Lissa's grip on the bowl froze and she stole a peek at Sullivan, as though doing so would help her concoct a plausible explanation—other than the truth, of course. Her parents were pretty old-fashioned.

"You're right, Donna." Sullivan's brows knit together. "Her face does look red and irritated."

The big oaf. At first, Lissa thought seriously about kicking him under the table, but refrained.

He knew perfectly well what had caused the light abrasion, but was playing dumb rather than acting guilty and drawing more curiosity. Could Lissa play the game as easily? She'd never been very good at that sort of thing. Maybe because she couldn't lie to save her soul.

She didn't feel the least bit guilty for what they'd done, even if it didn't mean anything to Sullivan. But she wasn't in the mood for a well-intentioned lecture after her lover went back to the guest house.

Since Lissa couldn't remember which cheek was red, she lifted her hands and touched them both. "I do feel kind of itchy. Maybe it's an allergic reaction to the makeup they applied at the salon."

"That's possible," her mom said, craning her neck to get a different look at the red, telltale splotch. "You might want to wash your face and apply some cortisone cream."

"Good idea," Lissa said, hoping the subject had died an easy death. "I'll do that after dinner."

Mom took a sip from her water goblet, then focused on Sullivan. "How are things coming along? Will you be ready for the reception two weeks from now?"

"We've got our work cut out for us, but I think we'll be ready. Of course, that means rolling up our sleeves and doing some of the physical labor ourselves." He shot a glance at Lissa. "Are you up to the task? More important, are you able to stay focused?"

Donna laughed. "You must not know my daughter very well. If anything, she's a workaholic and too focused on the business."

Are you able to stay focused? Lissa knew exactly what he meant. Could she stay focused on the task at hand, and not on pleasure? She had to. And fortunately, all the preparations for the Virgin Mist unveiling would keep them busy, which would help her keep up pretenses.

Of course, that didn't mean that each time she looked at him her heart wouldn't go topsy-turvy—like it was doing right now.

"Focusing will be easy," she said to Sullivan. "This reception and the unveiling is a high priority in my life. And I won't have any problem putting everything else on the back burner." Where it would undoubtedly simmer to the boiling point, if she let it.

"Good." Sullivan was glad Lissa knew what he meant, and that they were in agreement. He carried a ton of guilt over what he'd allowed to happen. It wasn't like him to let his libido take over his business sense and his good judgment.

Getting involved with Lissa wasn't a good idea. It complicated things. And it also distracted him with thoughts and urges best left for a less-complicated woman, best left to a time when he was off duty and prepared to play.

"Speaking of the reception," Donna said. "Which label did you two settle upon? I really like the artwork on that gold-and-black sample."

"I didn't think any of them were good enough," Sullivan said. "Not really."

"But won't you need to display the bottle for the unveiling?" Donna looked at Lissa, then back to him.

"I would have preferred to have the bottle or at least the artwork for the reception, but it's important that we choose just the right label, Donna. I don't want to sell Virgin Mist short. We can work around not having the finished product available by displaying the wine in the oak barrels, which only makes it look new and fresh."

"Well, I suppose you know best."

About marketing strategy and business? That was true. But Sullivan wasn't so sure about anything else.

For one thing, he'd always prided himself on being a good lover, a considerate lover, able to pleasure the woman in his arms. But that hadn't happened with Lissa. It hadn't been good for her, not as good as she deserved.

If she hadn't left his bed, he would have ended things by giving her an orgasm to remember. But as it was, Sullivan felt negligent, as though he owed her an earthmoving climax.

In his defense, he could argue that her virginity had surprised him. And so had her hasty departure. But that didn't absolve him from guilt.

At the time, after the last wave of his release and as his head cleared, Sullivan had worried that Lissa might make more out of their lovemaking than she should have. Especially with it being her first time and all. And to be honest, he really hadn't looked forward to having the standard, after-the-loving chit-chat with her—since it was tough letting a woman down easily.

But then she'd climbed out of bed and practically dashed out of the guest house, leaving him unbalanced.

He'd let her go and gone along with her let's-keep-things-casual, no-big-deal attitude.

It was over and done. End of story.

Yet something told him it wasn't over yet.

And for some reason, he wasn't quite sure whether he wanted it to be or not.

The act of indifference, as far as Lissa knew, had worked. Her mom hadn't picked up on the possibility that her oldest daughter had more than a business interest in the handsome consultant. And with each day that passed, Lissa grew more certain that her feelings for Sullivan were becoming personal and complicated.

Her dad arrived home, tired from his trip to San Diego and emotionally drained, but relieved to have his uncle's affairs in order and to have Uncle Pete in Oregon and settled in a private facility only twenty minutes away. If the hip healed sufficiently, God willing, and the doctors released him, they could bring the sweet elderly man home to live with them.

Dad had been pleased to know Sullivan and Lissa had carried on without him. And he'd been proud of their efforts to make the vineyard and winery look festive and inviting.

The landscapers worked double shifts all week. And yesterday, Lissa had gone to town and purchased a case of white twinkling lights to put around the trees that grew in the yard and up near the road. There'd been a ton of work to do, and both Lissa and Sullivan had jumped in to share it.

And now, as Lissa and her dad got ready for the first guests to arrive at the Virgin Mist reception, they surveyed the handiwork from inside the tasting room of the new winery.

They'd contracted the same caterer they'd used in the past. But this time, rather than choosing a wine to complement the meal, the woman had prepared appetizers and a menu that would enhance the taste of the wine they planned to launch.

''What do you think?'' Lissa asked her dad.

He slipped one arm around her waist, gave her a gentle squeeze and kissed her cheek. ''I think you're absolutely the most beautiful woman in the state. And I can't get over the change in you.''

''That's not what I meant.'' Still, she flushed at his compliment. The poor man had nearly lost his false teeth when he'd returned home to find Lissa in one of the short skirts and formfitting tops Jared had purchased. He'd also noticed that she'd let her hair down, something she'd refused to do in the past.

''I guess I should have taken you on a shopping spree years ago,'' he said, with a smile that seemed wistful and a little sad.

''Ah, Daddy. The makeover was long overdue. And if you'll remember, I always dreaded shopping trips in the past. Something just clicked inside of me.''

She didn't want him to think she'd cast him aside. Jared might have fathered her, but Ken Cartwright would always be her daddy—he'd earned that special place in her heart.

The heavy-set teddy bear of a man had given her

pony rides on his back until his knees had grown sore and red. And he'd stayed by her bedside whenever she'd been sick, unable to sleep until he'd known she was feeling better and was on the mend.

In fact, doting father that he was, he'd shared every single germ either of the girls brought home. He'd caught a mild but itchy case of chicken pox from Lissa, two bouts of strep throat from Eileen and every childhood illness that cropped up. And he'd never complained.

"I still feel as though I should have taken an interest in your shopping and stuff," Dad said, "like Mr. Cambry did. Your mom wanted me to, many times, and I should have put forth the effort."

"You didn't fail me in any way, shape or form, Daddy. The makeover had nothing to do with a man taking me into a dress shop." Her new look had more to do with the business consultant waiting at home, but she wasn't about to admit that to anyone. "It was just a matter of timing. I was ready to blossom."

"I want you to know something, honey. I love you—in the bud stage or fully bloomed."

He placed another kiss on her cheek, and she gave him a hug. "I know, Daddy. And I love you, too."

"You and Sullivan have done a great job with the unveiling. I just wish we could have displayed the bottled wine."

"We narrowed it down to three different labels, all of which were pretty good. But Sullivan wasn't happy with any of them. He says we need something better, something more intriguing.''

''That's why we brought the man in, honey. He understands marketing better than we do.''

Lissa agreed. So far she'd been impressed by Sullivan's business savvy and innovative ideas. ''He suggested, for tonight, that we display the oak barrels in a way that portrays the wine as fresh off the vine and something to be treasured.''

As the door opened, Sullivan sauntered into the winery wearing a tuxedo and looking like the heartthrob who starred in one of her more recent dreams.

With those red highlights in his brown hair, Sullivan still reminded her of a Scottish laird who'd traveled through time. And when he slid her an appreciative smile, dropping the business-like expression he'd hidden behind these past two weeks, her heart threatened to burst from her chest.

''You look great tonight, Lissa.''

''Thank you.'' She refrained from telling him he looked like a broadsword-yielding warrior on a windswept moor. And that she'd love to swing onto the back of his steed and ride off to his castle in the highlands.

Having sex was supposed to make those fantasies disappear, not make them more vivid, more intense. More complex.

Ken greeted Sullivan, then looked at his wristwatch before excusing himself. ''I'll be back shortly. I have to see what's taking my wife so long. The guests will be arriving soon.''

After he'd gone, Sullivan's eyes lingered on Lissa's hair, her face, her gown. ''That's a pretty dress. I like the color. And the fit.''

''Thank you.'' She wore an outfit Jared had purchased, a sea-green gown with a slit up the side for easy movement. Jared had said the men wouldn't be able to take their eyes off her, and she'd hoped he was right.

''I'm glad you didn't put your hair up again,'' Sullivan said, his gaze warming her from the inside out. ''I like it loose.''

She'd used pearl-and-silver clips to pull the sides of her hair back, but the remainder flowed down her back. And when Sullivan looked at her—his eyes filled with sexual awareness—she felt special, self-assured.

Before Sullivan had arrived at Valencia Vineyards, Lissa had felt confident about her knowledge, about her work as a vintner, about the blend she'd created. But thanks to Sullivan, she felt good about herself as a woman—one who'd touched the heavens.

She'd intended to steer clear of the handsome man this evening, to make him think that she didn't want to be at his side, that she didn't want more than she'd asked for. But after seeing the way he looked at her, she wasn't so sure that was the right approach.

Maybe, after the reception ended and the last guest

went home, Sullivan would be able to put business aside—one more time.

Because Lissa wanted another chance to touch the moon and stars, even if she couldn't call them her own.

As the evening progressed, Sullivan found it difficult to remain aloof and unaffected by Lissa's smile or the sparkle in her eyes as she made her way through clusters of people who'd come to Valencia Vineyard to celebrate the launch of Virgin Mist.

But it was pretty damn hard to keep his mind off the lady when she'd knocked the socks off every man at the reception. More than a few moved in on her, even some of the guys who'd brought wives or dates. Their words remained polite and cordial, but Sullivan could see the interest in their eyes.

They, too, were mesmerized by the metamorphosis.

Had they noticed the change in her personality, too? She appeared more confident. More daring.

She even carried herself differently than before, reminding him of the playful socialites he chose to date in an effort to keep his relationships light. Or at least, that's the excuse he gave himself for dogging her all night long, trying to keep the wolves at bay.

When Anthony Martinelli approached her by the display of oak barrels, Sullivan was hard-pressed to remain at a distance, so he moved closer, joining them.

"You've done a wonderful job with the reception,'' he heard the older man tell Lissa. ''And an even better job of creating a full-bodied wine sure to be a hit. Virgin Mist is delicate and rich, elegant and forward, fruity and complex.''

''Thank you.'' Her eyes brightened, setting off a display of emerald fireworks.

Martinelli nodded at Sullivan, acknowledging his presence, then resumed his conversation with Lissa. ''Have you come up with a label?''

''We're designing it now.'' She flashed Sullivan a smile, including him in the conversation.

''I suggest you consider a sketch, using your profile as a model.'' Anthony reached for a strand of her hair. ''Wearing it like this, of course.''

As much as Sullivan hated to admit it, hated to see the old buzzard fondle Lissa's hair and caress her with his eyes, the guy had a hell of an idea.

Sullivan could see the label now—an image of Lissa, with her Lady Godiva hair sparking a man's imagination, his thirst. A virgin walking in the mist.

It took all he could to keep from pulling her aside to let her know Martinelli's comment had set his imagination soaring, and that he had the perfect idea for the label.

''If you want the name of a renowned artist who specializes in sketching the human face, I'd be happy to give you a referral.'' Martinelli cast an appreciative smile at Lissa. ''The only thing drawing more attention from the wine this evening is the elegant vintner who created it.''

Sullivan wanted to clobber the guy for being so damn poetic and gallant. Lissa wasn't going to fall for that mush, was she?

Not that she didn't look hot. And not that her image wouldn't make a killer label for a dynamite wine. But Martinelli was too old to be making a play for her.

Hell, the vintner's interest in her had been obvious before, but now he was moving in for the kill.

Sullivan wanted to grab the guy by the lapel of his expensive tuxedo jacket and tell him to back off.

But Lissa wasn't Sullivan's woman. And Martinelli wasn't doing anything wrong. Not really.

It just didn't feel right to think of them together.

Maybe Sullivan still bore a trace of the old jealousy he'd been left with after his ex had left him for an older lover.

That was the only reason Sullivan didn't like the idea of Martinelli making a play for Lissa.

That and the idea Lissa might fall for the guy.

Two hours later, after the last guest had left and the catering staff had the bulk of the clean-up complete, Ken approached Lissa and Sullivan, where they stood beside a stack of oak barrels. "You both did an incredible job. The reception was a huge success."

"Thanks, Dad." Lissa turned to Sullivan and smiled. "I have to give our consultant a lot of credit for that. I didn't realize he would roll up his sleeves and get to work the way he did."

Normally, Sullivan left the physical labor to others.

But working side-by-side with Lissa had been tough, and he'd needed to exert some pent-up sexual energy. Besides, he also wanted Virgin Mist to get the kick-off it deserved. "Lissa put in more than her share of sweat, too."

"Well, I appreciate everything you did." Ken took Donna by the hand. "Hon, are you ready to turn in for the night?"

"Yes, I am. It's been a long day, and I'm exhausted." Donna turned to Lissa. "Did you want to walk up to the house with us?"

"If you don't mind," Sullivan said, "I'd like to talk to her about a few things."

"Certainly," Ken said, leading his wife to the door. "Good night."

When they were alone, Sullivan leaned against a barrel. "Martinelli had a good idea. You should be the model on the label."

"I don't know about that." Lissa scrunched her pretty face. "I don't want my image displayed on wine bottles."

"I'm not talking about a photograph, just a gold-embossed sketch. You'd be walking naked in the mist, your hair covering most of you."

She shot him an incredulous glance. "If you think I'd model in the nude, you're nuts."

He wasn't crazy at all. But she had a point. He didn't like the idea of her posing naked. The very thought of her removing her clothes in front of some-one else reminded him of the sensual striptease she'd done for him. And for some reason, he'd like to think of that as his own private show.

"The artist can put your face and hair on another woman's body," he said, unwilling to let her veto the idea.

"In that case, I'll consider it." She flashed him a playful smile. "I suppose we'll need to thank Anthony for the idea."

Sullivan didn't want to thank the guy for anything. "He only mentioned your face. I had the idea of incorporating the mist. And the naked body."

"I'll have to thank him tomorrow evening."

"Why tomorrow?"

"He asked me to go to dinner."

Dinner? A knot formed in Sullivan's gut. "And you accepted?"

She crossed her arms and lifted her brows. "Is that a problem?"

Uh-oh. Time to backpedal. He had no claim on Lissa. And he didn't care who she dated. It was just that the guy bothered him. That's all. "No. It's not a problem. You can certainly date whoever you want."

She eyed him carefully, as though she didn't buy his explanation or his fancy footwork. "You're not jealous, are you?"

"Of course not." If she wanted to date anyone else but Martinelli, it wouldn't have bothered him. At least he didn't think it would.

She studied him for a moment, as though she could

see something he couldn't. "You really don't like Anthony, do you?"

"No." But not because the guy had done anything wrong. He was just too old.

And too interested in Lissa.

She edged close to him, her peachy, orchard-fresh scent accosting him and setting off a flurry of pheromones.

His reaction should have scared him, but he didn't back away. And although he'd kept his thoughts to himself—for the most part—he slowly let down his guard.

What would she see in his eyes? Jealousy?

No way. Martinelli just reminded him of Kristin's lover, the guy she'd chosen over Sullivan.

Lissa placed a hand on his lapel, close to his heart. Could she feel the acceleration of his pulse?

"Was once enough for you?" she asked.

He'd thought so. He'd hoped so. But the fact was, he'd found it difficult to sleep in the bed they'd shared. Her scent had remained in the bedding for several days. And the image of her striptease lingered in his mind.

"Was it enough for you?" Believe it or not, he actually hoped she'd say no and complicate his work at the vineyard, at least one more time.

She smiled with both innocence and seduction. "I wouldn't mind doing it again."

With him?

Or was she thinking about Martinelli?

The past-his-prime vintner would probably be happy to take a pretty young woman like Lissa to bed, to kiss and stroke her to her first climax. But Sullivan wanted to be the one who saw that first orgasmic pleasure in her eyes.

Otherwise, she'd be comparing their first time to her next sexual encounter. She'd be comparing him to someone else. And he'd be damned if he'd let her think that Anthony Martinelli was a better lover than him.

Pride took over, and in spite of his better judgment, Sullivan took her in his arms and lowered his mouth to hers, claiming her.

Just for tonight.

Chapter Eight

Lissa leaned into Sullivan's embrace and lost herself in his kiss. She hungered for his taste, his breezy, highland scent, his touch.

As tongues mated and hands roamed, their breathing grew ragged and hot. The kiss intensified, playing upon her senses, fanning her desire.

Sullivan caressed her derriere with both hands, then pulled her flush against him. She felt his hard arousal, and nestled against it, letting him know she wanted him, too.

Lissa might have been inexperienced before, but not any longer. She knew what to expect, what she wanted. And what she needed to fill the ache of emptiness in her core.

Her pulse raced, and heat settled in her belly. She wanted to peel off his clothes—hers, too—and feel him skin to skin, breasts to chest.

Maybe they'd make love right here, in the tasting room, on the floor. And, interestingly enough, she found the idea of making love in the winery erotic. Exciting.

Besides, it would take too much time, too much effort, to walk across the grounds and into the cottage. And Lissa wanted Sullivan, wanted this.

And she wanted it now.

A loud clamor echoed in the room, alerting them both to the presence of someone else.

She tore her mouth from his, only to notice the assistant caterer stoop to pick up a stainless-steel pan he'd dropped onto the polished concrete floor.

"Sorry." The young man, his eyes wide and cheeks flushed, clutched the pan to his chest. "It slipped right out of my hands."

"No problem," Lissa said, although the annoying and embarrassing interruption had made her jump like a skittish cat.

The bungling caterer looked ready to bolt. And she couldn't blame the poor guy. The heated kiss he'd witnessed belonged behind closed bedroom doors.

"I…uh…left this pan behind." The young man nodded toward the door, moving backward for a quick escape. "I'll just let myself out. We're leaving now, if that's okay."

"Fine." Lissa looked at Sullivan, trying to read his

thoughts. Had he changed his mind? Not that he'd actually suggested anything, but that kiss had nearly sent her soaring through the rooftop, and she figured it had affected him, too. At least, she hoped so.

When the caterer shut the door, Sullivan raked a hand through his hair. "I guess I'd better walk you back to the house."

"Yours or mine?" she asked, afraid he'd send her home. To bed. Alone.

He blew out a heavy sigh. "Back to your house, now that I'm thinking straight. I don't have any more condoms, so that kiss will have to do until I can pick up a box in town."

"Remember when I went into town and purchased those little white lights?"

He nodded.

She slid him a slow, playful smile. "I stopped by the drugstore that afternoon. Just in case."

Just in case? Sullivan should have been concerned about her premeditated purchase, since he really hadn't wanted their relationship to go any further. But right now, in the blood-pumping afterglow of a hungry, insatiable kiss, he was glad to know they had protection at their disposal.

The condom they'd used before had been old. Maybe expired. So even if he had another one left, he wouldn't feel good about using it. He certainly didn't want to risk a broken rubber in the midst of passion.

And to be honest, Sullivan was glad that Lissa

wanted to make love again, glad that he had the chance to make things right—before any comparisons went into effect.

"So, where'd you stash the condoms?" he asked.

"I hid them between the box spring and the mattress in my room."

"We're not making love there." Not in her parents' house.

"I didn't expect us to." She crossed her arms. "I couldn't very well carry a box of condoms with me tonight. And I wasn't sure whether we'd need them or not."

"We'll need them." He ran the knuckles of one hand along her cheek, felt the silky-soft skin he'd marred last time with his afternoon stubble. "While you get the condoms, I'll shave. I don't want to leave any marks on you this time."

"It didn't hurt," she said. "And neither did the one you left on my breast."

He gently tugged at a lock of her hair, then let the silky strands slide through his fingers. "Well, I'll be careful this time." Careful to make sure she enjoyed it every bit as much as he did. Even more.

Sullivan took her by the hand and led her to the entrance of the winery, then waited while she turned off the inside lights and locked the door.

As they walked along the roadway, their feet crunched along the pavement, and an owl hooted in the distance. The fertile scent of farmland filled the crisp, nighttime air, and a blanket of stars cast a romantic spell upon the entire vineyard.

Sullivan slowed his steps near a young maple tree, its branches sprinkled with small, twinkling lights. He drew her to a stop.

"Tell me something. Were you planning another seduction?" His lips quirked, casting a crooked grin her way.

"You kissed me first," she reminded him. "I just wanted to be prepared."

"And I appreciate your foresight." He cupped her cheek. "Come on. Let's make it quick."

She stood on tiptoes and brushed a kiss across his lips. "Good idea."

Sullivan sure hoped so.

The only thing that seemed to matter was taking her back to his bed, bringing her unexpected pleasure, making things right. And after she'd cried out with fulfillment, he'd bury himself deep within her.

He wasn't going to worry about business and ethics until tomorrow, after they'd both been sated. Then, maybe he could get pretty Lissa off his mind for good. A heavy-duty relationship with her wasn't going anywhere. For more reasons than one.

And she seemed to know that, too.

Sullivan had a well-established and successful consulting business that required him to travel for weeks on end. And Lissa was firmly rooted on the vineyard. It was the perfect setup for infidelity and heartbreak.

And he ought to know. He'd seen it happen to his parents, and he'd experienced it firsthand.

It was best to keep things light. Unencumbered. And then he'd be on his way.

They crossed the small bridge and the lawn, but before they reached the steps of her front porch, she paused and said, ''I'll stay inside until I'm sure they're asleep.''

''Fair enough.'' He watched until she disappeared into the muted light of the quiet house. Apparently, she was determined to keep things a secret between them, as she'd said.

He was okay with that. It would make things less complicated when he left.

Taking a deep breath, Sullivan glanced at the crescent-shaped moon. Too bad it wasn't full. Lissa deserved the best that Sullivan *and* the night had to offer.

He turned and walked back to the cottage, where he would wait for Lissa to come to him.

Like a virgin in the mist.

An hour later, Lissa slipped out of the darkened house and headed across the lawn, toward the bridge that led to the cottage. She hadn't wanted her parents to know she was sneaking out to meet Sullivan. Not that she was doing anything wrong. But to be on the safe side, she'd waited until after they'd gone to sleep.

No need to worry them. Or to provoke any questions she didn't want to answer.

She'd taken off her dress, since she assumed it would end up in a wad on the floor. In its place, she'd slipped on a pair of flannel night shorts and a one-size-fits-all T-shirt. Unfortunately, her shopping spree with Jared hadn't included a skimpy nightie. And this was the best she could do.

It was chilly outside, so she'd put on a robe. As she neared the cottage, she contemplated running back home and changing her clothes. Surely, she could find something more alluring, more sexy than this.

But knowing her and the insecurities that had been known to plague her, she'd be hard-pressed to find something suitable. And by the time she settled on the proper garment to wear to a tryst, Sullivan would probably be sawing logs.

Soft light poured from the cottage window, as she approached. Rather than knock, she opened the door and let herself in.

Candles flickered on the coffee table. A fire glowed in the hearth, and a sensuous tune played on the stereo—Kenny G, at his best.

Sullivan sat upon the sofa in the cozy living room, wearing a pair of slacks and a lazy smile. No shirt. No shoes. No pretenses.

She flipped a strand of hair behind her ear, a little more nervous than she'd expected.

He stood, then moved toward her and took her hand. ''Want to sit by the fire for a while?''

No. She wanted to feel his arms around her, to taste

his kiss. But she nodded and let him lead her to the overstuffed sofa.

''Why don't you take off the robe?'' he asked.

She slipped out of the worn chenille housecoat and draped it over the easy chair. Then she took a seat beside him.

He took her hand and held it in his lap. His thumb made a slow circle on her skin, sending a warm rippling tingle along her arm. ''We rushed into things last time, and I intend to take it slow this evening.''

How slow? She wasn't sure whether she could wait patiently, without pouncing on him, trying to revive the heated kiss they'd shared in the winery.

The fire licked the logs on the grate in the hearth, while the sounds of a sexy instrumental filled the air. The ambiance heightened her senses, her sexual awareness. Her anticipation. And she realized Sullivan knew exactly what he was doing, where he was taking her.

The lovemaking had already begun.

He gave her hand a gentle squeeze, and she looked at him, caught the passion in his gaze.

Then he kissed her. Slow and gentle at first, but deepening the kiss until she thought she'd go wild. Desire nearly consumed her, and she ached to have him inside her, where he belonged—if only until the end of the month.

Somehow, and she wasn't entirely sure when, she ended up lying on the sofa, with him hovering over her, caressing her, taking her places she'd never been.

Sullivan wrestled with his desire, trying to keep it at bay, while he slowly removed her shirt, baring her breasts for him to caress and kiss. Her nipples had already beaded, and a flush crept over her chest—a sure sign that his efforts to arouse her had been rewarded. But he wouldn't stop the foreplay yet, wouldn't press for more.

They made out like a couple of teenagers exploring their sexuality, their bodies' reactions. And even though Sullivan had a lot of experience, he still found it exciting to learn what pleasured Lissa, to watch the passion glaze her eyes, to hear her whimper.

He used his hands and his mouth to bring her to the precipice of her first climax. And he nearly beat his chest in primal pride when the waves of pleasure took her over the edge.

"Oh, wow," she said, her eyes wide in awe. "I've read about those, but never had any idea it would be so nice."

"Nice?"

"Much better than nice," she said, a sated smile curling her lips.

"They'll only get better," he said.

"Next time?"

"As the night progresses."

Sullivan and Lissa made love on the sofa. And on the living-room floor. And finally, sometime before dawn, they found themselves on the bed, in a room lit only by lilac-scented candles Sullivan had found in the linen closet and used to set the mood throughout the house before she'd arrived.

He knew they'd both be wiped out tomorrow, as they tried to focus on the work still left to be done. But tonight he didn't care.

As they lay amidst rumpled sheets, among the blended scent of their lovemaking and fields of lilac, Sullivan ran a hand along Lissa's hip, taking time to savor the silky texture of her skin.

Lissa might be new to the world of sex, but she was a fast learner.

"I'd like to ask you a question," she said.

Uh-oh. His hand slowed, his fingers resting upon the edge of her thigh. "What do you want to know?"

"How do you feel about us having a discreet affair, one that'll end when you leave?"

Normally, he would have run for the hills at a time like this. But even though he was wary of entering a committed relationship, the one she proposed didn't seem too scary, especially since he had an out. He was leaving in two weeks—maybe less.

And she was only suggesting a short-term affair, which is all his relationships ever were.

If he told her no, he'd have a hell of a time keeping his hands to himself while they continued to work together. And quite frankly, he didn't want to. Not after the last mind-spinning climax they'd shared.

Funny, but the idea of a one-on-one until he left the vineyard didn't bother him—too much.

Some women got pretty territorial when it came to

the men they were sleeping with. Except, maybe, for the ladies he dated.

But Lissa wasn't like any of the women he'd gone out with in the past. And he wasn't sure whether that was a good thing or not. Still, he'd be a fool to think he could remain at the vineyard without wanting to make love to her again.

"A two-week affair?" he asked. "One we keep secret?"

She nodded.

"I think that can be arranged."

She smiled, green eyes dancing in the candlelight. He felt a tightening in his chest, just at the thought of having her to himself. Heck, he might even get a little territorial—for the next couple of weeks.

That was one way to put the kibosh on ol' Dapper Dad's program.

"What about Martinelli?" he asked, hating himself for doing so. But he wanted to hear her say the dinner date was history before it even started.

"What about him?" Lissa asked, tracing his eyebrow with her finger.

"Are you going to cancel your dinner plans?"

"Why should I?" she asked.

"Just wondered. That's all." He tried to keep the reaction from his face, the furrowed brow, the frown. The surprise. Disappointment, too.

Lissa was going out with the guy anyway?

She brushed a lock of hair from his forehead, her fingers lingering on his skin. "I know you don't like

Anthony, although I can't figure out why. It's only a dinner. Besides, you'll be leaving soon.''

And that meant she'd have another lover waiting in the wings.

Sullivan's gut knotted. But only because his successor might be Anthony Martinelli. That's the only reason.

He didn't want her to go, but what was he supposed to say? *I want you to myself?*

No way. Sullivan wasn't into promises and commitments. Not with women.

Not even when the lady looked as good as Lissa and fit so nicely in his arms.

Besides, his work here would be over soon. And if she was taking the affair this casually, all the better for him. All the easier his leaving would be.

So why did he still feel like clobbering the old guy?

Like a masochistic fool, Sullivan sat on the porch of his cottage, waiting for Martinelli's car to pull up. He still couldn't believe Lissa hadn't called off the date. Hell, she'd even left the vineyard office early to get ready.

And here he was—babysitting the darn dog like a lovesick clown.

What kind of deal was that?

In the wee hours of the morning, before she'd left to sneak back into her house, Sullivan had again asked her if the dinner was still on. He'd expected her to tell him she would call Martinelli and cancel.

After all, it didn't seem right to spend the night making love with one man, then go out to dinner with another when the sheets were hardly cold.

"Anthony and I have known each other for years," she'd told him. As if that negated what Martinelli had up his sleeve.

"We're just friends," she'd added.

Oh yeah? Well somebody ought to tell the old buzzard that. Martinelli wanted more from Lissa than friendship.

The puppy growled, then barked and tugged on his new yellow leash, trying to get Sullivan's attention. Barney wanted to go for a walk near the pond, as they'd done in the past. But Sullivan wasn't going anywhere.

He preferred to stew on the porch about something that shouldn't bother him at all.

When a champagne-colored, late-model Lexus pulled up, Sullivan tensed his jaw. He watched as Martinelli climbed from the car and headed to the house, all decked up in a classy suit. Suave and sophisticated. Tall and lean.

The guy looked good for his age. Too good. He probably had a gym in his house. And steered clear of fats and carbs.

Sullivan grumbled under his breath. Maybe he ought to just take the dog for a walk, watch Barney chase one of the old ducks that waddled in and out of the pond.

If Lissa weren't in danger of falling for another old duck, he would.

Well, hell. Someone had to look out for her. She might have lost her virginity, but she was still innocent, as far as Sullivan was concerned.

He'd unleashed a lamb into the wild, so now it was his responsibility to look after her.

And for that reason, he planned to sit right here until Martinelli brought her home.

Chapter Nine

Lissa peered at her reflection in the mirror and sighed at the sight of puffy, dark circles under her eyes. They really didn't surprise her. She'd spent most of last night in the cottage with Sullivan, which had left her sexually fulfilled, but exhausted.

She glanced at her wristwatch. Nearly five-fifteen. Anthony would be here any minute, if he wasn't downstairs already. She probably should have canceled the date with him. And she wasn't entirely sure why she hadn't.

Maybe because Sullivan expected her to. And maybe because she didn't want her lover to think she was making more out of their relationship than it was, or that she expected more than he was willing to give.

There was, of course, another reason she'd agreed to go out with Anthony. Other than that high-school fiasco with Milt Preston, Lissa had never been on a real date before.

Besides, Sullivan would be leaving soon. So where would that leave her? She had a life to think about, a future.

"Lissa," her mom called from the living room. "Anthony is here."

She took one last glance at the mirror, then headed downstairs. She'd chosen the same black dress she'd worn to the dinner party, rather than one of the more stylish outfits Jared had purchased. She looked all right—and certainly not like a woman who was having a heated affair on the sly.

A yawn slipped out, as she entered the spacious living room, where her mother and Anthony chatted on different sides of the sofa. She would definitely have to make this an early night.

"I'm sorry to keep you waiting," Lissa told Anthony.

"No problem." He stood and cast her a charming smile. "You look lovely."

"Thank you."

His gaze caressed her and lingered longer than was appropriate for a business dinner. She might have downplayed his romantic interest before, but she saw it now. Clearly. Sullivan had been right—about Anthony's interest in her, but not about his character.

Anthony Martinelli was a very nice man. Too old

for her, she supposed. But a good conversationalist. And handsome.

Who knew what might develop down the road. Wasn't that why people dated? To learn more about each other? Of course, in Lissa's case, she still had a lot to learn about herself—at least in affairs of the heart.

She turned to her mother, wondering whether her mom had picked up a vibe that this evening was a date and not at all business-related.

Mom merely smiled at the old family friend. ''I hope you two get a chance to enjoy the meal, Anthony. Lissa has been so focused on Virgin Mist that she hasn't taken any time for herself.''

Apparently, her mother thought bags under the eyes were the result of burning the midnight oil and not from making love until dawn.

''Shall we go?'' Anthony asked.

''Do try to have some fun,'' her mother said, as she walked them to the door.

''I'll make sure of it, Donna.'' Anthony placed a gentle hand upon Lissa's back and escorted her out of the house and to his car.

''How do you think your parents will feel about us dating?'' he asked, as they approached the top-of-the-line Lexus.

So, there it was. Out in the open. This was definitely a date.

''I'm not sure how they'll feel, Anthony.'' For

some reason, Lissa wasn't concerned about her parents' reactions right now.

But shouldn't she feel at least a tingle of excitement at his interest?

She glanced at the guest house, where Sullivan sat on the porch, and gave a little wave to acknowledge him. He didn't act as though he'd seen her, but she suspected he had. And the scowl he wore told her he wasn't a happy camper. Was he grumpy because he disliked Anthony? Or was it more than that?

A niggling sense of guilt swept over her.

Okay. So maybe she should have feigned a headache and canceled.

But it was too late now.

"I thought we'd have dinner on the coast," Anthony said. "I hope that's all right with you."

"It sounds nice." Lissa hadn't made the thirty-mile drive in ages. "I didn't get a lot of sleep last night, though. So I'd better warn you. I might start winding down early."

"I'll try not to keep you out too late," Anthony said, appearing a bit disappointed but understanding.

Just before six o'clock, they arrived at Café Europa, the restaurant Anthony had chosen. Lissa found the small, intimate dining room with white plaster walls and dark wood beams quaint and appealing.

The maître d' greeted Anthony like a favored customer, then sat them at a linen-draped table that displayed a crystal votive and a vase of tulips. A large bay window provided a majestic view of the rocky bluff, as well as the ocean.

"This is one of my favorite places to dine," Anthony said, as he took the seat across from her.

"I can see why. The atmosphere is incredible."

During the cocktail hour and dinner, Anthony was a perfect gentleman. And they spent a pleasant hour or two in conversation.

"How was your salmon?" he asked.

"It was wonderful. And so was the service. I'm surprised there isn't a line waiting to get in."

"Not many people know about this place—yet. But word will spread." He scanned the interior. "I like the European flair."

She smiled. "The atmosphere suits you."

"It suits you, too." A smile crinkled his eyes, yet he still didn't look his age.

When the waiter returned with the processed credit card, Anthony added a tip and signed the receipt. "I suppose I'd better get you home."

"That's probably a good idea." She'd hate to fall asleep in the car. He might think that she found him boring, which wasn't the case.

He reached across the table and took her hand. "You know what they say about all work and no play."

Yes, she did. After the reception, she and Sullivan had played all night long. But that would remain her secret. "As soon as we've officially launched Virgin Mist, I'll consider a vacation."

"Good." He smiled and released her hand. "Are you ready to go?"

"Yes. Thank you. I had a wonderful time." And she had. All in all, the evening had been much nicer than she'd expected. But she was glad it was over.

Nearly forty minutes later, they pulled into Valencia Vineyards and followed the long drive to the house. As Anthony parked, Lissa looked at the darkened cottage.

Apparently, Sullivan had gone to bed. He had to be as tired as she was. Maybe more so. She'd dozed off once or twice last night, in a pleasant afterglow. And each time she'd opened her eyes, she'd found him wide awake, watching her.

Anthony slid from the driver's seat, then circled the car and opened her door. "I have tickets to the theater next Saturday. And I'd like you to join me."

He took her hand and helped her from the car. His manners impressed her, flattered her. But that didn't mean she felt good about going out with him again. Not while Sullivan was still working for the vineyard and living on the property. And even after Sullivan moved on, she suspected his memory would hold her back as well.

"I'm going to be pretty busy with Virgin Mist for the next couple weeks," she said. "Maybe another time?"

"Of course."

Again, she glanced at the darkened cottage. If truth

be told, she was glad Sullivan had turned out the lights and gone to bed. It made things easier that way.

Who needed to hear an "I told you so," even if it came from her own conscience?

She'd just leave Barney at the guest house and talk to Sullivan in the morning.

At the front door of the family home, the porch light glowed in a golden welcome.

"Would you mind if I kissed you?" Anthony asked.

The question took her aback, and she wasn't sure what to say. In a way, she wondered how Anthony's kiss would compare to Sullivan's. The only other kiss she had to measure it by was the wet and sticky one she'd shared with Milt Preston on this very porch.

"No, I wouldn't mind."

With a debonair smile, he took her in his arms and lowered his mouth to hers.

It was a nice kiss, cloaked in the fresh fragrance of his musky aftershave. It was a gentle kiss, soft and sweet. All in all, the kiss was pleasant, but it lacked the heat and passion of Sullivan's.

"I'll call you in a few days," Anthony said.

"All right."

He smiled, then turned and walked away. As she watched him go, her gaze drifted to the cottage, where the outdoor light suddenly came on. And a dark figure took a seat on the deck.

What had Sullivan been doing? Sitting in the dark?

Well, it wasn't dark any longer. And she had a feeling the scowl he wore had never left his face.

As Anthony drove away from the vineyard, Lissa headed for the guest house to get Barney. She wasn't in a hurry, though. Something told her she'd be in for a lecture. Or a sullen pout.

Okay. So the date had been a mistake. The kiss, too. But rather than reveal her regret and disappointment, she forced a smile and continued to walk.

Maybe Anthony Martinelli *was* too old for her. Maybe he'd been a family friend for so long she'd never be able to think of him as anything else. But a more likely explanation was that she wanted to see fireworks and feel the heat she'd recently grown accustomed to.

How many more men would she have to kiss before finding one who made her heart flutter and her body sing the way Sullivan did?

Sullivan had dozed off in the chair shortly after Lissa left. And he'd awakened only moments ago.

He hadn't purposely turned the lights off. He just hadn't gotten up to turn any of them on. Not even after Martinelli's car pulled up.

And like a voyeur in the dark, Sullivan couldn't help but watch the couple from his seat on his deck.

Lissa had kissed the guy. And not just a peck between friends.

All right. So it wasn't the kind of kiss that got a man's blood pumping, but Martinelli was too suave to press for more on the first date. But that didn't mean the middle-aged vintner didn't want more from her. Or that he wouldn't make a bolder move next time.

A sense of betrayal washed over Sullivan, although he wasn't sure why. He and Lissa hadn't made any lifetime promises. So he suspected it was some of the leftover baggage from his divorce that made him want to throw a punch or two at the salt-and-pepper-haired vintner.

There was no other reason for Sullivan's senseless resentment. So why did he feel an ache in his gut and a hole in his chest?

He watched as Lissa made her way across the lawn and over the bridge. All the while, he sat.

And waited.

"Thanks for looking after Barney," she told him, as she stepped onto the deck.

"You're welcome."

She took Barney from his lap and held the puppy in front of her, like a shield, while the little pup wiggled and squirmed to give her a couple of wet kisses on the chin. "I guess I'd better take him home."

"Are you coming back?"

"Not tonight. I'll see you in the morning. I need to get a good night's sleep."

Sullivan needed a good night's sleep, too. But he doubted he'd get one.

And he cursed under his breath for letting her go without a fight.

* * *

The next day, neither Lissa nor Sullivan brought up the subject of Anthony Martinelli, the dinner date or the disappointing kiss.

Nor did they mention making love to each other again.

Instead, they focused on work, on marketing, on ads and television commercials.

Still, getting back in Sullivan's good graces—and in his bed—was never far from Lissa's mind.

"I've asked an artist to meet us tomorrow morning," he said.

"An artist?"

"To sketch the image of the virgin for the label." He leaned back in his chair. "You're not going to back out, are you?"

"No. I guess not. But you said just my face, right?"

He slid her a playful grin, his gaze warming her straight to the core. "That's what I said. But another female model might not do your body justice."

Her cheeks warmed. And so did her heart. The tension between them was easing, which was good. She didn't like the idea of dealing with Sullivan on a strictly business level.

"Then maybe I ought to pose," she said, wondering if the decision would irritate him. Especially since she suspected the kiss she'd shared with Anthony had annoyed him, even if he never mentioned it. "Are you sure it won't bother you if I do?"

"No. It won't bother me a bit if you strip down in front of the artist."

She found that surprising. And disappointing. The couple of times she'd suspected Sullivan might be feeling a bit jealous had actually pleased her. Not that she wanted him to be a bossy and possessive brute. But maybe, deep in her heart, she hoped their relationship wouldn't be shallow and based only upon lust. Of course, that didn't mean she wouldn't be realistic about the future of an affair destined to end when his job was done.

"I didn't know you'd already started scouting an artist," Lissa said. "Where'd you find him?"

"Her." Sullivan tossed Lissa a crooked smile. "The artist I want to use is a woman. I thought you'd be more comfortable."

Or would *he* feel more comfortable?

Lissa was probably reading *way* too much into this, but it felt good to think Sullivan might be a wee bit territorial about their relationship, their intimacy.

"All right. I suppose modeling in the nude won't be so bad after all." Lissa stood to stretch the muscles that kinked in her neck, then moved to the window to peer outside.

What she needed was some exercise, some fresh air. Being cooped up in the office for days on end was getting to her.

As she walked, a squeak sounded when she stepped on something small and rubbery. Barney had left one of his chew toys in the middle of the floor.

"Hey, Barn, you'd better come get your rubber duckie." She scanned the office, but didn't spot the little rascal. Where'd he go? "Barney?"

Sullivan, who sat at the desk, looked up from the ad layout he'd been working on. "I haven't seen him since this morning. Maybe he curled up and fell asleep."

They scouted around the office, looking in every nook and cranny. But Barney was nowhere to be found.

"Maybe he slipped outside when your mother brought us sandwiches and iced tea," Sullivan said.

"I'd better go look for him." She strode to the door, with Sullivan on her heels.

Twenty minutes later, they still hadn't found the puppy. They'd checked the pond, where every unruffled duck and swan was present and accounted for.

"I don't know where else to look." Lissa tried to keep the worry from her voice, but she'd become very attached to the playful, loving little dog.

"We'll find him." Sullivan nodded toward the house. "Maybe he followed your mother home."

As they neared the side of the yard, the gate was open. Sullivan pointed. "There he is. By the garden shed. But it looks as though he's gotten into something."

"Imagine that," Lissa said. Barney had a penchant for mischief. But as she drew closer, she noticed a frothy green coat of saliva on his snout.

She picked him up, holding him at arm's distance

so the goop wouldn't stain her blouse. "What did you eat?"

Sullivan pulled open the shed door and peered inside. "Bad news. Look." Sullivan pointed to a chewed up box of rat poison.

"Oh, my God. No." She hugged the puppy close, no longer worried about her blouse.

"Come on," Sullivan said. "I'll take you to the vet."

An hour later, Sullivan drove Lissa home. Each time he glanced across the seat and saw her tear-stained cheeks, he wanted to reach out, to comfort her.

"Barney's so little," she said, capturing his gaze. "Do you think he'll be all right?"

"The vet said he'd know more in the morning. I'm sure pumping his stomach will help. It just depends upon how much he ingested before we found him. And how much his body absorbed."

"I know this may sound crazy to you, but I've really come to love that little guy. And I don't want to lose him."

Sullivan knew exactly how she felt. When he was a kid, he'd had a dog who'd been his best friend and his constant companion. In fact, Bandit had been there for him when his parents' marriage hit the rocks, when going home after school would have been otherwise unbearable.

"I've grown pretty attached to the pesky little guy,

too,'' Sullivan said. ''Pets have a way of burrowing their way into our hearts.''

Lissa sniffled, then let out a sob. The tears began to flow all over again.

Sullivan may not have been comfortable with emotional stuff, but he knew how it felt to lose a pet. And how it felt to have no one understand that kind of grief.

He remembered the day Bandit had died, the day he'd cried himself sick. The day his dad had said, ''That's enough, son. Go wash your face and dry your eyes.''

Easy to say, and tough to do when the pain kept twisting a kid's heart and wringing the tears right out of him.

Unsure of what more he could say or do, Sullivan let her cry until they returned to the vineyard. Then, after parking the car, he went around to help her out. He wasn't trying to mimic Martinelli's style and manners. It was more than that. Lissa was pretty torn up about her pet, and he wanted to help. To support her. Or whatever. He wasn't too good at this sort of thing.

As she climbed from the car, he slipped an arm around her, and she leaned into him. He held her while she cried, something he wished his overbearing dad had done. Couldn't the man have understood that a brokenhearted nine-year-old couldn't just suck it up when his family had fallen apart and the only one who seemed to give a damn about him was a dead dog?

"I'm sorry for being such a crybaby," she said. "I don't usually fall apart like this."

"Don't be sorry. I understand."

Did he? Lissa clung to Sullivan, to his strength, his support. The sexy man could turn her inside out with a smile and send her heart soaring with a kiss. Yet now, he stroked her back in a gentle, understanding way. Funny, how her body knew the difference—appreciated the difference.

His compassion touched her. Even more than his flirty smile, quick wit and easy laugh.

If she ever fell in love with a man, she'd want him to be the kind who would stand by her through life's ups and downs. A man who would hold her when she cried, as Sullivan was doing now.

"Want to go to the cottage for a while?" he asked. "Maybe have a glass of wine on the deck?"

She nodded. "Yes. I'd like that." She didn't feel like returning to the office. Not when her heart and mind were at the veterinary clinic with Barney.

As they walked, Sullivan reached for her hand. "I lost my dog when I was just a kid. Cried for three days and refused to go to school."

She sniffled. "What was his name?"

"Bandit. He was just a mutt I'd found wandering the neighborhood. But he was the best friend I ever had. My only friend, for a while."

"What happened to him?"

"He used to meet me at the school bus stop every afternoon. And one day, he wasn't waiting for me at the curb.'' Sullivan took a deep breath, as though reliving his own grief. "So I called him. He came flying out of the neighbor's yard and dashed into the street. Right in front of a mail truck."

"I'm sorry." She gently squeezed his hand, while wishing she could do more.

When they entered the guest house, Sullivan closed the door. Then took her in his arms and gave her a warm, gentle kiss.

How could he do that? Give her a heated, body-arousing kiss one minute, then one that was comforting and heartwarming the next?

"My folks never understood the depth of my grief," he told her. "They bought me a puppy, a golden lab with champion bloodlines. For some reason, they thought they'd replaced Bandit with a better dog. But they hadn't."

She wrapped her arms around him, trying to absorb a little boy's pain, trying to share her own.

He brushed a kiss across her brow, then gazed into her eyes. They stood that way for a while, caught up in a powerful bond. Something passed between them, something warm and mesmerizing. Something Lissa wanted to hold close to her heart forever.

Was it love?

It had to be.

Without words, without needing any, Sullivan led her into the bedroom, where they undressed, slowly and deliberately. Their joining was gentle, soothing and stirring. And when he entered her, she arched to meet him, taking all he had to offer and giving all she could in return.

The loving rhythm built to a powerful peak, bursting into a star-shattering climax that rocked her heart and soul.

Lissa wanted to say the words, to tell Sullivan what she truly believed—that she'd fallen in love with him.

But she held her tongue and closed her eyes, relishing the moment, the warmth and intimacy. Savoring the aura of promise that surrounded them.

Their relationship had taken an unexpected turn this afternoon. At least it had on Lissa's part.

Did Sullivan feel it, too?

She hoped so. Because the realization that she'd fallen in love with him both touched and frightened her.

What if he didn't feel the same thing for her?

Letting him go after his job at Valencia Vineyards had ended would tear her up.

Especially if he walked away from her without a backward glance.

Chapter Ten

Long after Lissa left the bed in the guest house and went home, Sullivan lay still, staring at the ceiling.

He always held something back while making love. And he'd never let go like that before. Not even with his ex-wife.

That didn't mean sex with Kristin hadn't been good. It had, at least in the early stage of their marriage. But somewhere along the way things had changed. He'd opened his heart and closed his eyes, blinding himself to reality.

Until he came home that stormy day in November and found Kristin gone.

She'd left a note that was supposed to make him understand why things hadn't worked for her. For them. But her words only brought on a rush of pain, anger and resentment.

Instead of providing answers, her rambling explanation had merely provoked more questions: Why hadn't she wanted to face him? Why hadn't she mentioned her unhappiness sooner?

Even now, Sullivan still wasn't sure exactly when their marriage had gone to hell.

But he knew the affair he and Lissa had embarked upon had just taken a downhill slide.

While making love with Lissa, he'd opened up his heart—this time, just a crack—and closed his eyes. And that's when it happened, when he got that sinking feeling in his chest. The forewarning of disaster.

He wasn't sure how Lissa felt about their little "fling," as she called it. But on his part, there'd been more than lust going on. How much more, he couldn't be sure. But it was enough to scare the liver out of him.

That kind of intimate release led people to ask for promises others couldn't keep, commitments that would only lead to heartbreak and disappointment.

Been there. Done that. And Sullivan wouldn't make the same mistake, wouldn't set himself up for emotional suicide again.

Who was he to think that the career of a traveling consultant would be conducive to a stable relationship? And what about Lissa?

She was on a light-hearted quest for self-discovery.

Why else would she dangle Martinelli on a string while sleeping with Sullivan?

The telephone on the nightstand rang, and he answered.

"Hello," Donna said, her voice as sweet and gracious as ever. "Dinner will be ready in about ten minutes. We're having spaghetti tonight."

Sullivan didn't feel like eating. Not at the family table. The Cartwrights were slowly sucking him in. Making him comfortable. Too comfortable.

He couldn't let that happen. "If you don't mind, I'd like to have dinner alone tonight. I've got another client, one I'll be working with when I finish here at Valencia Vineyards. And we need to have a telephone conference. It'll take quite a while."

If there was anything to the Pinocchio tale, Sullivan's nose would have sprouted a couple of feet by now. Not that he didn't have a client to talk to. But the conversation would take all of three minutes.

"That's too bad," Donna said. "But I understand. I'll have Lissa bring you a plate of food."

"Don't do that," Sullivan said a little too quickly. A little too panicky. "I'm not really hungry this evening."

"Are you sure?" she asked.

"Positive."

He had to pull back. To cut his losses and get out while he could.

After all, Lissa was interested in Martinelli. And

with Sullivan's luck, he'd open his heart to the beautiful, green-eyed Lady Godiva and she'd walk away.

Just like his ex.

And if there was one thing he'd learned through his parents' crappy marriage and the painful reinforcement he'd received from his own marital breakup, it was to keep a sexual relationship light. Unencumbered.

Sullivan had to keep his eyes wide open, if he planned to keep his heart in one piece.

Early the next morning, before Lissa left for the office, the phone rang.

"Honey," her mom called from the kitchen. "Can you get that? I'm wearing rubber gloves. And I'm up to my elbows in oven cleaner, grit and grime."

"Sure." Lissa answered in the hall.

"Miss Cartwright?" an unfamiliar male voice asked.

"Yes."

"This is Doctor Margolis at Hidden Valley Veterinary Clinic."

Her heart dropped to her stomach. "How is Barney doing? Is he going to be okay?"

"He's much better this morning, although not completely out of the woods. Of course, he doesn't like the charcoal we've been giving him to absorb the poison. But he seems to be on the road to recovery."

"Oh, thank goodness." She blew out the breath she'd been holding. "When can he come home?"

"I'd like to keep him just a bit longer. Why don't you pick him up after lunch?"

"Thanks, Doctor. We'll be there around two o'clock."

We'll be there?

It was a natural assumption, wasn't it? Sullivan would probably want to go with her. After all, he'd been worried about Barney, too.

Did she dare hope that they'd taken a step toward being a real couple? It sure felt that way yesterday afternoon when he'd supported her through Barney's ordeal. And when he'd made tender, mind-spinning love to her.

Of course, when he hadn't joined them for dinner last night, her old insecurities had flared, suggesting he might be pulling away from her. But she quickly dismissed them. After all, Sullivan had a conference call to make, another client he needed to speak to. And Lissa understood that.

Still, as she'd stared at his empty seat, felt the loss of his heart-tingling smile, she'd realized how difficult it would be to let him go, once his job at Valencia Vineyards was finished. But that didn't mean he wouldn't come back.

Lissa and Sullivan had found something special, something worth holding on to.

Hadn't they?

"Who was it?" her mother called from the kitchen.

"It was the vet. Barney is doing better."

Before Lissa reached the front door, the phone rang again.

At this rate, she'd be late to meet Sullivan at the office. She sighed heavily, then grabbed the receiver from the lamp table near the sofa. "Hello."

"Lissa? It's Jared."

The call took her aback, but only for a moment. She'd talked to the man after the reception, when he'd called to ask how everything went. But she didn't think he'd called to chat today. "Hi, Jared."

Did he have the results of her blood test? Would she be able to donate bone marrow to Mark?

"I have some bad news," he said.

"I'm not a match?" She couldn't imagine any news that would be worse than that, other than a setback in Mark's condition. She said a quick prayer, hoping that wasn't the case.

"No." His voice sounded rough and ragged. "You're not a match."

"I'm really sorry." The words seemed so hollow, so insignificant. But not because they weren't sincere. She knew what this meant to Mark, to Jared, to everyone who loved the little boy. They'd have to search for an unrelated match. And that narrowed their chances of finding a bone-marrow donor in time.

"And there's something else," Jared said. "The paper work we found at the Children's Connection indicated Olivia's child had a different blood type than the lab reported for you."

Her heart went out to the poor man. The records

he'd found had been painstakingly pieced together. But that left all kinds of room for error. "Maybe you were mistaken, Jared. I might not be your daughter after all."

"Actually," he said, "the preliminary tests indicate you are my daughter, but that's where things get confusing."

"What do you mean?"

"Originally, I came to the vineyard looking for Adam Bartlite. His name was listed on one of the scraps of paper we'd found in the salvaged file. Your address was on a different piece. I put those two bits of information together when I shouldn't have."

Obviously. But she understood his desperation, his need to find a donor for his son. "Jared, I'm still not following you."

"There was yet another scrap of charred paper in the file. One that listed the blood type of a child born to Olivia Maddison."

"And my blood type doesn't match that one?" Lissa furrowed her brow. "I don't understand. My parents were told my mother's name was Olivia. And that was before the fire destroyed any of the paperwork."

"I think Olivia may have given birth to twins who were separated at birth—a boy and a girl. Although it's rare, you have different blood types. Your brother was adopted by another family. And his name is Adam Bartlite."

"Are you sure?"

"No. But I intend to find out."

Lissa leaned against the side of the sofa. Her life had certainly taken a strange twist. Once the adopted daughter of Ken and Donna Cartwright, her family had grown to include Jared, his wife and three half siblings. And that wasn't all. She might have a brother. A *twin* brother.

"I didn't mention this before," Jared said, "because I didn't think it was relevant. But multiple births run in my family. And Olivia told me she'd had a twin who died as an infant."

"I'm stunned," Lissa said. "To say the least."

"Me, too. But a twin birth is the only possible explanation."

"And now you need to find Adam," Lissa said.

"Yes."

Her *real* brother. Did he look like her? Did they share any of the same mannerisms? The same likes and dislikes? Had her twin been blessed with a loving home, as she had?

"I'd like to meet Adam," Lissa said. "When you find him."

"It may take some time. I just came to this conclusion this morning, after the doctor called to give me the lab results. But I'll keep you posted."

"Thanks, Jared. And if you need any help looking for Adam, I'll do what I can."

"I appreciate that."

When the telephone disconnected, she stood in the

living room for the longest time, trying to sort through things.

There'd been a lot of changes in her once simple life. Her family was growing by leaps and bounds, assuming Jared was right about her having a twin brother.

And then there was Sullivan. Lissa couldn't wait to share the news with the man who'd become so much more than a lover. Did she dare dream that they might create a family of their own?

By the time she arrived at the office, Sullivan was busy working on another ad layout. He glanced up from the desk, no doubt wondering what had kept her. After all, she was never late to work.

"What's up?" he asked.

"Good news and bad. First of all, Barney is doing much better. And the vet thinks he'll make it."

"That's obviously the good news. What's the rest of it?"

She adjusted her hair, then sat on the edge of the desk. "I'm not a match for Mark, Jared's son."

"That's too bad." Sullivan leaned back in the tufted leather desk chair. "What happens now?"

"Well, Jared has reason to believe I might have a twin brother out there someplace. And he's trying to find him."

Before she could go into any further explanation, the office telephone rang.

Now what? She wondered, unable to quell her impatience. Or a sense of dread.

She lifted the receiver and tried to. command an upbeat voice. "Valencia Vineyards."

"Lissa, this is Gretchen Thomas with *Through the Grapevine* magazine. I'm sorry about not being able to make it to the reception last Saturday night."

"That's all right," Lissa said, glad the woman hadn't been in attendance. She didn't think she could have stood by watching the reporter make goo-goo eyes at Sullivan. "Sometimes things don't work out. I understand."

"Well, my boss was at the reception and was very impressed with what you've created. He believes Virgin Mist is going to be well received by consumers and connoisseurs alike. So he suggested I do a bigger spread on both the wine and the vintner."

"That's great," Lissa said, although her enthusiasm was muted by the fact she couldn't donate bone marrow to her younger brother. And also by the possibility that she had a twin. Somewhere. For the first time in her life, she found it difficult to focus on business.

"So if you don't mind," Gretchen said, "I'd like to make an appointment to come out to the vineyard and interview you."

"Sure." Lissa glanced at Sullivan. She wasn't excited about watching the reporter flirt and fawn over the man she was sleeping with, the man she loved. But the publicity would be good for the vineyard and Virgin Mist. "When did you want to come out here?"

"The sooner the better. If I can get a photographer

to accompany me, I'd like to set something up for this afternoon.''

"That'll be fine," Lissa said, although she'd rather send Sullivan on an errand that would keep him busy until after the blond bombshell had left the premises. Maybe he could go get Barney at the vet—without her.

If she scheduled it right…

"Should we aim for one o'clock?" Gretchen asked.

The vet was out for lunch between twelve and two. So much for orchestrating Sullivan's absence. But the article was too important. And Lissa's jealousy was silly and misplaced. After all, Sullivan hadn't given the busty blonde much attention when she'd made a play for him at dinner. "Sure, Gretchen, one o'clock will work out fine."

"I think Roger, my photographer, is free, but I'll confirm as soon as I know for sure."

When Lissa hung up the phone, she told Sullivan what Gretchen had said.

"Having the editor of a wine magazine think that highly of Virgin Mist is a real plus. I guess we'd better turn on the charm when Gretchen arrives."

That's what Lissa was afraid of.

Sullivan would turn on the charm. And since his work at Valencia Vineyards was coming to an end, Gretchen would lure him into her eager arms.

Sullivan tried hard to keep his mind on his work. He needed to tell Lissa that their affair was over. That it was best they end things before he left—which, by the way, would be next week. Hell, maybe sooner than that. Some of the loose ends could be handled over the telephone.

But he thought he owed her more than an It's-been-nice-knowing-you. He wasn't sure just what he owed her, though. More than the Dear John he'd come home to find—that was for sure.

He supposed having an adult conversation over a glass of wine on the deck was better than a discussion over a scarred-oak desk in a stuffy office, so he decided to wait until the workday was over.

Of course, Lissa had been the one to suggest the temporary affair in the first place. And she *was* interested in Martinelli. It was possible that she wouldn't give a rat's hind end if they each went their own way in the next couple of days.

And maybe their lovemaking yesterday hadn't affected her in the same way it had him. She could have been so caught up in emotion over her concern for Barney, that she hadn't felt the same intimacy that he'd felt. The same gut-wrenching fear of getting in too deep.

"Is something wrong?" she asked, when he peered out the window for the fifth or sixth time since the clock had struck one.

"No." He was just edgy. Unsettled. And waiting for the cavalry to arrive.

Where the hell was the *Through the Grapevine*

magazine reporter? She'd take the focus off what had happened between Lissa and him. Although Sullivan still wasn't exactly sure what *had* happened between them.

"Are you looking for Gretchen?" Lissa asked.

Maybe he was. But the tone of Lissa's voice indicated female concern. Jealousy?

"She's late," is all he said. "And you have to pick up Barney."

"Did you want to go with me?" she asked.

"I have some work to do later this afternoon. And I have to schedule my next client."

Her face dropped, and her brow furrowed. Disappointment?

Since when had he not been able to read a woman's expressions and at least have a good idea what she was thinking and feeling?

At a quarter past one, a white van with a grape logo on the side pulled up, and Gretchen Thomas climbed out. Tight-fitting jeans clung to the curves of her hips, complementing her long legs. And a form-fitting pink T-shirt displayed her other assets to their fullest.

Damn. That woman was proud of her figure. Too proud, if you asked him. But that didn't mean he didn't appreciate looking at her.

He shot a glance at Lissa, saw her lean against the desk with her arms crossed and fix a solemn look on her face.

Anger? Hurt? Or was she merely disinterested?

Hell, he didn't know for sure. Working with Lissa after yesterday's killer bout of intimacy-in-the-buff left him uneasy.

Hey, maybe she thought he was acting strangely. And *that's* what he'd read in her expression.

"I'll get the door," Sullivan said. Then he invited Gretchen inside, along with her sidekick, a pudgy male photographer who seemed to be enamored with the sexy reporter. *Good luck, pal. She's way out of your starry-eyed league.*

"It's nice to see you again, Sullivan." Gretchen extended an arm in greeting, giving his hand a warm, lingering squeeze.

"Same here." He still preferred not to mix business with pleasure, but he had a feeling Gretchen wouldn't let that stop her.

"Hello, there." Gretchen slid Lissa a smile, as though finally noting the vintner she'd come to interview. Noting the makeover, too, he suspected. But she didn't acknowledge the change in Lissa.

"This is my photographer," Gretchen said, nodding to the short, stocky man. "Roger Donaldson."

While the men shook hands, Gretchen withdrew a small tape recorder, a pen and a pad of paper from a black canvas tote bag.

Lissa took a seat at the desk, and the reporter sat across from her.

"All right. Let's get started." Gretchen placed the tape recorder on the table and jabbed at the record button. "Tell me, Lissa, what made you want to become a vintner?"

"I've always admired my father. As a small child, I tagged along after him every chance I got. He taught me a love for the land and the vineyard. And naturally, I followed in his footsteps."

Gretchen quickly got down to business, asking questions, scribbling answers. Sullivan had to give her credit. She seemed to know her stuff. And he suspected the magazine spread would be well-written, with the wine and vineyard presented in a positive light.

"How about a tour?" Gretchen asked.

Lissa glanced at her wristwatch. "Sure. As long as we can get it done within the next half hour. I've got an appointment at two."

"I'm sure it won't matter if you're late," Sullivan said. "As long as you get Barney picked up before the vet closes, it should be all right."

Lissa nodded, then led Gretchen and Roger outside. Sullivan followed several steps behind.

Nearly two hours and two rolls of film later, Gretchen seemed pleased with what they'd accomplished. Sullivan had tried to keep a low profile, and surprisingly enough, the reporter had performed like a professional—until she closed her notepad and stuck it in the canvas bag she carried.

"So," Gretchen said, sidling up to Sullivan and slipping her arm through his. "How much longer will you be on the clock?"

''A couple of days or a week. I'm not sure yet.''
He looked at Lissa, trying to gauge her reaction.

Surprise, then indifference? Or was the lack of interest merely an act?

Hell, it didn't matter. They had to have that talk soon. Maybe tonight.

''When you're on your own time and free to pursue a little pleasure,'' Gretchen told him, ''I'd like to take you to dinner.''

''Sure. I'll have time when my work here is done.'' Sullivan shot another glance at Lissa, saw a stonelike mask on her face. He hadn't really meant to encourage Gretchen. Or to anger Lissa. But he'd just done both.

He certainly wasn't about to beat himself up over it, though. He and Lissa needed a change of pace.

The intimacy mode he'd slipped into yesterday added to his unfounded jealousy of Martinelli, proving that Sullivan had let things with Lissa get way out of hand.

He slid a look over his shoulder, spotting Lissa walking alongside the photographer. She didn't appear troubled or worried. Maybe she'd come to the same conclusion as he had—that it was time to end things between them.

But the nondescript smile she wore didn't provide any clue as to what was on her mind.

Lissa had been shocked when Gretchen had asked Sullivan out to dinner. And even more so when he accepted.

Of course, the two lovers hadn't acted as though they were anything more than a business consultant and his client, so she really couldn't blame the pushy reporter for stepping on invisible toes.

But that didn't mean Lissa wasn't hurt.

When Sullivan looked over his shoulder and caught her eye, she feigned a smile, hoping to hide the ache inside. He was leaving in a week. Maybe in days. And he hadn't broached the subject with her. Hadn't even asked whether she'd like to keep seeing him.

Gretchen's aggressive style rubbed Lissa the wrong way. But a dagger of grief sliced deep into her chest when Sullivan agreed to go out with the pushy blonde. And not even the afternoon sunshine or the fertile scent of grapes growing on the hillsides could lift her spirits or ease her pain the way it usually did.

They strode two-by-two along the dirt roadway that led to the office, where the magazine's van was parked. Gretchen had taken hold of Sullivan's arm. And Lissa was left to bring up the rear with sweet, chubby-cheeked Roger, who was huffing and puffing like a little choo-choo train saying I-think-I-can, I-think-I-can.

Maybe it was time to end things with Sullivan. But she feared it was too late.

Lissa had fallen head over heels for the playboy business consultant who would soon leave her and her heart in the dust. Like he was doing now.

As they reached the office, Lissa spoke to both

Gretchen and Sullivan. "If you'll excuse me, I need to go pick up my puppy from the vet."

"That's fine," Gretchen said. "I have everything I need from you."

Yeah. And now it was time for the busty reporter to procure what she *needed* from Sullivan. But Lissa refused to let her feelings rise to the surface—not in front of anyone.

In the past, she'd spent a lot of time alone, usually because she was more comfortable staying close to home and out of the limelight.

But this was different, she decided, as a cold cloak of loneliness settled around her. And she knew it would be worse when Sullivan actually packed up his things and drove away.

She entered the office and grabbed her purse, but before heading to the car, she went into the bathroom to freshen up, to wash the emotion from her face.

The paper towels were nearly gone, so she bent to get another roll from under the sink. And there, sitting front and center, was the package of feminine napkins she kept handy—pads she'd be needing soon.

Soon? Her hands froze on the cupboard door, and her mind reeled as she began to count backward.

She was late. About a week. Maybe two. And she'd always been regular. Could she be pregnant? With Sullivan's baby?

Surely not. They'd used condoms.

There had to be an explanation—like anxiety. Lissa

had been under tremendous stress recently, with the unveiling of the wine. And from meeting her biological father. Even the excitement of having sex for the first time might have postponed her cycle.

That had to be it. She shut the cupboard door, leaving the roll of paper towels under the sink. She had to get out of here. Had to get to the vet. And to the pharmacy in town.

Those home pregnancy tests were pretty accurate, or so the ads said. And a negative result would do her nerves a world of good.

The sooner she put the fear of pregnancy aside, the better off she'd be. Lord knew she had enough to worry about, enough to deal with.

Besides, Barney needed her—even if Sullivan didn't.

She peered out the office window, scouting a swift escape. Roger waited in the van, while Gretchen continued to chat with Sullivan. His back was to the office door. So taking that moment to slip away unnoticed, Lissa averted her eyes and quickly jumped in her car. Tears threatened to give way, but she blinked them back.

You're getting way too emotional about this, she told herself, as she backed out of the parking space, threw the car into Drive and headed away from the vineyard.

What do you mean, *too* emotional? She'd fallen in love with a man who was slowly pulling away from her. And it hurt more than she could have imagined.

What a fool she'd been.

She'd only meant to lose her virginity. Losing her heart hadn't been part of the plan.

And what if she'd gotten pregnant with Sullivan's baby?

Could things get any worse than that?

Chapter Eleven

An hour later, Lissa returned to the vineyard with Barney. The puppy had whined, piddled on the vet's floor and gone absolutely bonkers when he saw her, which made her feel slightly better.

At least someone loved her back.

She parked her car where the van had once been, then scooped Barney into her arms. Thank goodness, the magazine people had left. It would have been nearly impossible to keep her emotions in check if she'd had to watch Gretchen throwing herself at Sullivan.

When Lissa entered the office, Sullivan looked up from the paperwork on the desk. He broke into a grin at the sight of a wiggly Barney in her arms. ''How's that little rascal doing?''

"You'd never know he'd had a brush with death or that he'd had his stomach pumped yesterday." Lissa placed the squirmy pup on the ground and watched him scamper toward his basket of toys.

Sullivan leaned back, the desk chair squeaking in protest. "You know, I think we've done the bulk of the work that needs to be done on the premises. We can probably handle the rest by telephone or e-mail."

Lissa didn't need a psychic to see what was happening. Sullivan was leaving—and ending things. And he was trying to be cool and casual about it. Well, she'd play it his way. Or at least, she'd try to. "Whatever you think would work best."

"I think I can wrap up things here in another two days. Claire is coming tomorrow, and we'll need another full day after that. So let's plan on me leaving by mid-morning on Friday." Sullivan fiddled with the ink pen on his desk, then caught her eye.

Did he see her disappointment? Her heartbreak? She managed a flimsy smile in response. She didn't trust her words to get past the knot in her chest.

"I don't see any need to charge you for on-site consulting when I can advise you from my home office for a nominal fee."

Lissa should probably feel grateful, but she didn't. His leaving might be good for the vineyard—financially speaking—but it was tearing her up inside.

"I appreciate you looking out for our best interests," she said, trying to assume a nonchalant stance, even though her heart and her world were spinning out of control.

She'd never been a good actress, so she made her way to the window and peered out at nothing in particular. The vineyard had always provided her comfort and peace before. Would that continue to be the case, now that Sullivan had come and gone from her life?

It didn't seem likely that things would ever be the same again. She certainly wouldn't be.

"By the way," Sullivan said. "Claire Windsor called while you were at the vet. She's the artist I'd like us to use for the sketch. I've tentatively scheduled a sitting, but wanted to run it by you first."

Lissa, with her back still to the man she loved, stared blankly through the pane of glass. "Whatever you decide is fine with me."

"Don't you want to know more about her? Maybe take a look at her Web site and see a sample of her work?"

"That isn't necessary." She turned and, while leaning against the windowsill, crossed her arms. "You've done the research. Besides, that's why we hired you. For your expertise."

Their relationship had gone back to business mode. And even if Lissa didn't like the way things had turned out, she'd do her best to remain strong. Unaffected. In control.

"Claire can come out tomorrow morning, if that's

okay with you. Otherwise, she's not available until late April or early May."

"Then tomorrow will have to do."

"That's what I was thinking. The sooner we get that label designed and under production, the better."

Yes, and the sooner he would be able to cut all ties to Valencia Vineyards, all ties to her.

The artwork on the label was the only thing pressing—and probably the only thing he felt responsible for, since he hadn't liked any of the samples she and her dad had shown him.

"What time is Claire coming?" Lissa asked.

"First thing in the morning, if I give her the okay." He studied her, as though trying to figure out what she was thinking, feeling.

But she'd be damned if she'd give him a clue. "Then go ahead and confirm, Sullivan. I'll be glad to have the label finished and the wine bottled."

"Great. I'll send her an e-mail and give her directions."

They worked a while longer, their conversation focused on business. But things between them were strained, at least that's how it felt to Lissa.

Some of the strain might be self-inflicted, she supposed, since her thoughts kept drifting to the home pregnancy test locked in the glove compartment of her car.

As soon as Sullivan went back to the cottage, she'd retrieve the test, follow the instructions and put her fears to rest—once and for all.

Maybe then she could get used to living without Sullivan in her life.

She glanced at the clock on the wall. Five-oh-seven. Her mom would be calling soon, reminding them it was time for dinner.

"Are you going to eat with us this evening?" she asked, somehow knowing he wasn't. But as his client and host, she thought it was best to ask. To assume nothing had changed their business relationship, that their lovemaking had never taken place.

"No, I'm not going to be able to join you. I already called your mom and told her. I have some errands to run in town, and it will be easier if I pick up something to eat while I'm gone."

She nodded, realizing he might not have left the vineyard, but he'd already left her.

The lovemaking they'd shared yesterday, the joining she'd thought had meant something special, had merely been his way of saying goodbye.

Lissa couldn't complain, though. She'd gotten what she wanted, what she'd thought she'd wanted—just a one-time fling. And apparently, that's all it had been to him. A fling. A temporary affair. A roll in the hay.

Unfortunately, that fling had meant the world to her.

"I think we can discuss the spring tour schedule in the morning, if that's okay with you." He stood and stretched.

She watched as his muscles flexed, realizing she'd never see him again. Never hold him. Never share a heated kiss or another earthshaking climax wrapped in his arms.

A dull ache grew in her heart, and she tried desperately to ignore it. She gathered her tattered emotions and tucked them deep in her chest. "I see no reason why we can't call it a day."

"All right. Then I'll see you in the morning." Sullivan made his way to the door, but when his hand gripped the knob, he paused and looked over his shoulder. "Maybe tomorrow afternoon, we can sit on the deck and discuss other things over a glass of wine."

Other things? Was he going to actually broach the subject of their…affair, or whatever? And if so, did she even want him to? Maybe it was better to let the whole thing die a humane death.

"I'm not sure there's anything to discuss," she said, trying to gain some kind of upper hand on their breakup, trying not to reveal she was dying inside.

That way, when he left, she'd have her pride intact. As well as the memory of their lovemaking to haunt her dreams.

He merely nodded, as though he agreed, as though they had nothing to talk about, which was just as well. The growing pain was nearly unbearable, and she feared the tears would begin to fall before he left, betraying the secret of her broken heart.

Grief lodged in her throat, preventing her from talking. But there really wasn't anything to say, anything to do—other than let him go with all the grace and indifference she could muster.

As the door shut, leaving her and Barney alone, Lissa remained standing like a stone-cold statue with missing limbs. And when she was sure Sullivan had made it into the guest house, she went to the car and removed the small brown bag that hid her purchase.

Once she'd safely locked herself inside the bathroom, she opened the box and pulled out the instruction sheet. Her hands trembled as she set up the plastic apparatus that would display the results. And when she completed the test, she waited.

And waited.

According to the instructions, a little pink dot would form if she was pregnant. So she stared at the small plastic contraption, the seconds pounding out in an agonizingly slow tempo.

Nothing yet.

Thank goodness. She glanced in the mirror and blew out a shaky breath. At least she didn't have to fear telling Sullivan that their little "fling" had left him a father.

She looked down at the pregnancy test one last time and gasped. What was that? Something pale and pink? No, it couldn't be. A dot?

They'd used condoms for goodness' sake. Had they gotten careless? Had one of them sprung a microscopic leak? Lissa knew those things weren't foolproof. But why did *she* have to be a statistic?

Lissa snatched the instruction sheet off the countertop. Maybe she'd read something wrong, done something wrong.

But no such luck.

The proof was in the bright-pink dot that glared back at her.

Still, there might be a mistake. These store-bought tests couldn't possibly be 100 percent accurate all of the time.

In the morning, she'd call the doctor and try to get in to see him, maybe ask for a more extensive lab test.

But deep in her heart, she had a feeling the pink dot wasn't a fluke. And that stress hadn't caused an upset in her hormonal balance.

Somehow, she'd gotten pregnant.

So now what? Did she dare tell Sullivan the news?

Or did she keep her secret to herself and let him leave without a backward glance?

Claire Windsor arrived at the vineyard office just after nine o'clock the next morning. She was a petite woman, with short, dark-brown hair, expressive blue eyes, and a ready smile.

Sullivan thought the stylishly dressed artist looked a lot prettier in person than she did in her Web site photo. The bright turquoise linen jacket she wore made her blue eyes sparkle.

Because of the awards, honors and achievements listed on her site, he guessed her to be about forty or so, although she didn't really look it.

"Did you have any trouble finding the place?" he asked.

"Not at all. Your directions were easy to follow."

When Lissa, who'd been taking Barney for a walk on a leash—or maybe it was the other way around—entered the office, Sullivan introduced the women.

"I can see what you mean," the attractive, forty-something artist told Sullivan, while studying Lissa's face. "She has a perfect profile for what you have in mind. And that hair? Beautiful."

"You came highly recommended," Sullivan told the artist. "I'm glad the timing worked out for all of us."

"I thought you got my name from my Web site," Claire said. "Who can I thank for the recommendation?"

"Anthony Martinelli."

The woman seemed taken aback at the mention of Anthony's name, but her expression eased into a smile. "It's been a long time since I've seen him. Our paths don't cross often. How is he?"

"Maybe you ought to ask Lissa," Sullivan said. "She's the one who knows him best."

Lissa flashed him a narrow-eyed glare. She was annoyed at him, most likely, and wanted him to know. Then she turned a cordial smile to Claire and addressed his comment. "Anthony lost his wife about a year ago, Claire. It was unexpected and a big shock. But he seems to be doing well."

"He's dating again," Sullivan interjected, unable to help himself from throwing a jab.

The vintner sure seemed to bring out that raw bone of jealousy in Sullivan, making him irrational. It shouldn't matter what Lissa did or who she dated. Sullivan didn't want a lasting relationship with her, but for some reason, he didn't want Anthony to have one with her, either.

Lissa crossed her arms and arched a brow. "When did you speak to Anthony about the artwork?"

"At the reception," Sullivan said, realizing he'd better do something to lighten her mood. "Anthony was the one who first suggested having your image sketched on the label. And he mentioned knowing a great artist. Don't you remember?"

"Now that you mention it, I do."

"So when you agreed to the idea, I found his name in your Rolodex and called him. He didn't have Claire's number, but he gave me her name, and I checked out her Web site. I was impressed by her work, so I set up the appointment." Sullivan slid the attractive, older woman a warm smile. "Anthony was right. You've got a lot of talent, Claire. And you'll do justice to both the lady and the wine."

"I appreciate your confidence." Claire turned to Lissa. "Should we get started?"

"Would it be okay if we did this in my bedroom?" Lissa asked.

"The Cartwrights have a beautiful garden," Sullivan said, thinking Claire would find the backdrop inspiring.

Lissa shot him an incredulous look. "I'm not taking my clothes off outside."

"Sullivan suggested I come out to the vineyard," Claire said, "since you might not feel comfortable in my studio. So I'll set up wherever you like. I can improvise the background in my workshop when I complete the project and prep it for use on the label."

"I'd feel better in my room," Lissa said.

"That'll be fine." Claire smiled warmly. "I'll go and get my things so we can get started."

When the artist had gone back to her car, Lissa crossed her arms and gazed at Sullivan. "So you called to get a recommendation from Anthony. Isn't that odd, considering you don't like the man?"

"I can put aside my feelings for the benefit of my client." Sullivan shrugged. "Besides, maybe I was wrong about the guy. You obviously think the world of him. So go ahead and date him."

"I don't need your permission or your approval."

No, Sullivan realized, she didn't. And for some reason, in spite of his determination to end things while his heart was still in one piece, he didn't like the idea of another man sleeping with her. Any man.

After the women walked out of the office, leaving Sullivan with Barney, he and the dog wandered to the pond. He wasn't sure how long he stayed out in the fresh air and sunshine with only Barney to keep him company. An hour? Maybe two?

He'd wanted to stay nearby, to make sure the sketching session went well. Or maybe it was just curiosity about the entire process.

About the time he decided only a fool would continue to hang around a duck pond with a goofy little pup who couldn't stay out of the mud, a champagne-colored Lexus drove up.

Anthony Martinelli.

What was he doing here?

The older man climbed from his car and approached the pond. He nodded toward the muddy pup chewing upon the bright yellow leash. "Part of your job description?"

Sullivan didn't think the guy was trying to be a smart aleck, but the comment grated upon him just the same, and he didn't see any reason to respond.

"I stopped by to see Ken," Martinelli said. "Is he home?"

"No. He and Donna went to see his uncle in the convalescent home. They should be back shortly."

Martinelli nodded, then glanced up. "Did you ever get in contact with Claire Windsor?"

"As a matter of fact, I did. She's here today."

"Oh, really?" Martinelli glanced toward the house.

Before either of the men could say anything more, Lissa walked out the front door, followed by Claire, who carried an oversize black canvas bag over her shoulder, a large black attaché case in one hand and a sketchbook in the other.

Martinelli flashed Claire a warm smile, and when

she shuffled the items she held, he took her hand in greeting. "It's good to see you again."

"It's been a long time." Claire removed her hand, but not her gaze.

That guy sure was suave. Too suave. What was he going to do? Hit on the artist, right in front of the woman he'd been dating?

"I'd love to see the finished product," Anthony said to Claire.

Sullivan tensed. He couldn't really blame the guy for wanting to see the sketch of Lissa without her clothes on. He wanted to see it, too. But Sullivan wasn't nearing the dirty-old-man age. And he wasn't trying to juggle two women at a time.

"Do you mind if I show them?" Claire asked Lissa.

"I guess I'd better get used to people seeing it." Lissa looked at Sullivan, then at Anthony.

Well, Sullivan minded. He didn't want Martinelli ogling Lissa—not even a sketch of her—and he had half a notion to grab the sketchpad and hang on tight. But that was crazy. Her image would soon be on every bottle of Virgin Mist wine.

Still, he wanted to sneak a peek. He wanted to see if the image captured the Lady Godiva essence he remembered.

Okay. So it was good. Innocent, but sexy. And when Claire took it home and finished working on it, the label would probably be dynamite.

"This is great," Anthony said. "You haven't lost

your touch, Claire. I can't wait to see the finished product.''

The finished product? Or the real thing? Just watching Anthony gaze at the drawing of Lissa's body tore at Sullivan's gut.

He had to get out of here before he made some stupid, lame, adolescent comment.

''I've got a couple of important calls to make in the office,'' he said, handing Barney's leash to Lissa and excusing himself.

As he strode across the grass, he realized he'd neglected to tell Claire she'd done a fine job capturing the beauty of Lissa's body.

But maybe that's because he was so caught up in the fact she'd caught that same innocent yet sensual expression Lissa had worn the first time they made love.

Lissa watched Sullivan leave, then returned her attention to Anthony and Claire, just in time to see the artist and the vintner exchange a private glance.

It appeared as though the two had a history of more than friendship. And she found her curiosity piqued. ''How long have you and Anthony known each other?''

''We met nearly twenty years ago, but have only seen each other sporadically,'' Claire said, tossing Anthony a charming smile. ''And we've had this…what would you call it?''

''An attraction,'' he said. ''Don't you think?''

Claire smiled. "I guess you could call it that. We met at the wedding of a friend, and Anthony asked me out. But I was leaving the next day for art school in New York. And by the time I returned, he'd married someone else."

"But our timing has always been bad. We've never been single at the same time." Anthony's gaze lingered on Claire. "By the way, how is Derek doing? The last I heard, he'd made a fortune on that business venture in Chicago."

"Derek had to travel a lot—for business purposes. Or so he said. Eventually he found a home away from home. The divorce will be final next week."

"I'm sorry to hear that." Anthony turned to Lissa. "Well, I guess I'd better go."

"I'll tell my dad you came by."

Anthony nodded, then reached into his jacket pocket and pulled out a business card. He handed it to Claire. "Let me give you my number. We've got some catching up to do."

Oh come on, Lissa thought. Who was the man trying to fool? He'd just found out that he and the woman he'd been attracted to for years were, for the first time, both single at the same moment.

But it didn't bother Lissa. Not at all.

Anthony and Claire were probably better suited to each other anyway.

Besides, Lissa wouldn't date the charming vintner again. Not if she was carrying Sullivan's baby.

And even if she weren't pregnant, a relationship with Anthony wasn't going anywhere.

Bottom line? His kiss hadn't measured up to Sullivan's.

And Lissa feared no other man's ever would.

Chapter Twelve

The next afternoon, Lissa went directly to her room following a visit to the doctor's office, where she'd learned an unsettling fact.

The home pregnancy test she'd purchased had been more dependable than the condoms she and Sullivan had used. And she was definitely going to have a baby.

Fortunately her folks had gone to visit Uncle Pete, so they weren't home to question her about her health or about why a workaholic would leave the hired business consultant to fend for himself in the vineyard office.

She lay on the bed, fully clothed, her hands resting upon a tummy that would expand with the growth of her child. She turned her head and studied the telephone, wondering if she dared make the call. She felt the need to share her news with someone.

But she wasn't yet ready to level with her mom and dad. Or her sister, who had managed to follow the rules and get married before getting pregnant.

She'd tell them all, of course, but not yet. She couldn't bear to see the disappointment in their eyes. Or the pity.

But there was one person whose image kept creeping into her mind. Someone who might care about her dilemma yet was far enough removed to offer wise counsel without making her feel like a fool.

Did she dare call Jared?

Talking to him might quell the overwhelming urge to bare her soul to someone. She rolled to the side, pulled out the drawer on her nightstand and withdrew the business card Jared had given her. What would it hurt?

He'd said to call him anytime, day or night. Had he meant what he said?

She sat up in bed, grabbed the telephone and jabbed a finger at the numbers that would reach him at his law office.

"Cambry, Ames and Walker," a woman said.

"May I speak to Jared Cambry, please? This is Lissa Cartwright."

"One moment. I'll see if he's available."

Lissa didn't have to wait long. Jared picked up almost immediately. "Hey, Lissa, it's good to hear from you."

Thank goodness. She felt a bond of some kind with the man who'd fathered her. And she was glad to know he'd felt something, too. She was getting awfully tired of one-way relationships.

"How's Mark?" she asked.

"He's pale and not as energetic as he used to be, but his spirits are good. And in spite of all the needle pokes, he doesn't complain."

Lissa's heart went out to the man and his family. Watching a bright, happy child grow ill had to be heart-wrenching. "Have you had any luck finding Adam?"

"Not yet. But I've got my investigator working on it."

Her desire to meet her twin brother had been heightened by the need to find a bone-marrow donor in time. And she now understood a part of what Jared had been feeling when he came to the vineyard. He'd wanted to find her after moving back to Portland, but Mark's condition had made finding her critical.

"How is the rest of the family holding up?" she asked.

"We're all trying to keep positive and upbeat around Mark, but it's been tough on us, especially my wife." Jared blew out a heavy breath. "Other than that, everyone else is doing well. And they're looking forward to meeting you."

"I'm glad," Lissa said, before lapsing into silence.

"Okay. What gives?" Jared asked. "I've been a dad long enough to know when someone has a problem and needs to talk."

What would Jared think of her when she told him she'd gotten pregnant and wasn't going to marry the father of the baby? Would he, considering his past mistake, understand?

There was only one way to find out. "I'm pregnant, Jared."

"Pregnant? That's great. Isn't it?"

A tear slipped down her cheek, and she swiped it away with the back of her hand. "I'm going to be an unwed mother."

He didn't speak right away. And she hoped it wasn't because she'd disappointed him. Maybe he was trying to think of something supportive to say. Something wise. Something that would make her believe everything was going to be all right, even if she was hurting to the bone.

"I didn't know your birth mother very well," he said. "But she once told me something I've never forgotten. And if she were alive, I think she'd tell you the same thing."

Lissa sniffled. "What's that?"

"Babies are a blessing."

"Is that how she felt about me?" Lissa hated being a mistake, an inconvenience, but she always tried to keep those old insecurities locked deep inside. So as a second thought and a cover-up, she added, "I mean, is that how she felt about being pregnant?"

"Olivia was only sixteen and not ready to be a mother," Jared said. "But she was willing to do whatever it took to provide her baby with a loving home, whether that meant keeping you herself or giving you up so that a loving family, like the Cartwrights, could have you."

"I've always wondered about her. About you, too. But she didn't have to carry me to term. And I'm glad to know she made me a priority in her life." Lissa blew out a soft sigh.

Her baby would be a priority, too. And fortunately, she was far more capable of providing financially for her child, something sixteen-year-old Olivia hadn't been equipped to do.

"I'm sorry that neither Olivia nor I were there for you when you were growing up," Jared said.

"I understand," she said, although a small, raw part of her was still trying to come to grips with him not being a father to her. But the fact was, she'd been raised in a loving home and had no complaints. "I had a wonderful childhood."

"You have no idea how happy I am that the Cartwrights raised you. I'll be grateful to them for the rest of my life. What did they have to say about your news?"

Lissa bit her lip. "I…uh…haven't told them yet."

"Why not?"

Because I'm afraid I'll disappoint them, afraid they'll think less of me.

Gosh, those old feelings were hard to shake. Lissa

was still competing for a place in their hearts, a place right alongside Eileen. "I guess I just wanted to bounce it off you first."

"I'm glad you did. But you also need to share this with your mother, when you're ready, of course. It didn't take me long to see how much that woman loves you. And I'm sure your father does, too."

Lissa nodded. "Yes. And you're right. I do need to talk to them about it. I guess I'm just afraid of letting them down."

"Kids have been disappointing their parents for years. And I'm sure your parents' reactions won't be as bad as you expect. And if they are? They'll get over it. Parents have been doing that for years, too."

"What made you so wise?"

"Disappointing my parents," he said. "And the lectures I had to listen to afterward. And the hugs and tears that followed. It's part of life."

"And speaking of life, I think I'm going to love having you in mine," she said, not quite ready to tell him she loved him, but knowing someday she would.

"I'm glad, Lissa. Just out of curiosity, what did the father of the baby say when you told him?"

She bit her lip and glanced at the antique beveled mirror over her dresser, spotting a lonely stranger staring back at her. "I haven't told him. And I'm not sure whether I will."

"You owe it to the man to tell him."

"It was just an affair. You know. A casual fling." Lissa closed her eyes and blinked back the tears. She hated referring to what she and Sullivan had shared as nothing special when it had meant so much to her.

"I didn't like hearing that Olivia was expecting a baby," Jared said. "Our relationship had been a one-night stand. But I wouldn't have wanted her to keep it a secret. She did the right thing by telling me."

"Thanks, Jared." Lissa wound the telephone cord around her finger, then added, "Just for the record. It was much more than a one-night stand for me. I fell in love with him, but he doesn't feel the same way."

"I'm sorry you're hurting."

"Yeah. Me, too. But that's how we gain wisdom, right? Disappointing our parents and ourselves?"

"And taking responsibility for our mistakes and trying not to make the same ones again."

He was right, and she was glad she'd called him. "I'll tell my mom and dad. And I guess I'll have to tell the baby's father, too."

"You've got me in your corner, Lissa. For whatever that's worth."

"It's worth a lot, Jared."

When the call ended, Lissa hung up the phone and blew out the breath she'd been holding.

In spite of her efforts to enter a no-strings-attached affair, she had fallen helplessly in love with a self-proclaimed bachelor who had no intention of settling down and would probably cringe at the thought of being a father.

But it wasn't her baby's fault. And Lissa would do

everything in her power to make sure her child knew how loved she or he was.

She'd tell her parents the news, of course. And in spite of her reluctance, she'd tell Sullivan, too.

He'd be leaving in the next day or so.

Leaving her forever.

But Lissa wouldn't be alone. She'd have his baby to love.

A child who would depend upon Lissa to make the world a special, loving place to live—even without a father.

"You've been especially quiet this evening," Donna said, as she and Lissa stood over the sink doing the dinner dishes.

"I've got a lot on my mind." Lissa reached for a wet plate from the drainer and wiped it dry. "I'm sure once the label is ready for the bottles and the first group of tourists arrive, I'll be fine."

Her mother bought the explanation, which was a relief, since Lissa didn't feel like talking.

"I sure hope the doctors release Uncle Pete and let him come live with us," Donna said.

"Me, too." Lissa's dad spent a lot of time at the convalescent hospital, trying to make his uncle comfortable after moving from the home he'd lived in for more than fifty years. "Then they could have watched tonight's basketball game here."

Her mom tightened her lips and worried her brow.

"I know. I hate having your dad on the road tonight, especially with that storm coming."

"Daddy is an excellent driver." Lissa placed a hand on her mom's shoulder. "I'm sure he'll be fine."

"You're probably right. But I worry just the same."

They went back to their work and, in no time at all, had the dishes put away and the kitchen back in order.

"I have some chocolate cake left over," Mom said. "Do you want to take a slice to Sullivan?"

Did she? That would give her an excuse to go to the cottage and speak to him about the baby, about the future. With him leaving tomorrow morning, she wouldn't have much chance to talk to him on a casual level.

"All right. I'll take him a piece of cake." Lissa folded the dishtowel and set it upon the clean countertop.

"I'm going to miss that man when he leaves," Donna said. "He sure was nice to have around."

Lissa was going to miss him, too. Not the cool, withdrawn businessman, of course. But she would always remember the charming, witty man who had been her first lover.

Mom handed her a slice of cake on a plate covered in plastic wrap. "Your dad probably won't be back for another hour, so I'm going upstairs to read for a while."

After wiping up the few chocolate crumbs from the counter, Mom rinsed out the dishcloth and draped it over the faucet. "Be sure to take a jacket and umbrella. That storm should hit pretty soon."

Lissa nodded. "I will."

"See you in the morning, Lis." Her mom gave her a kiss on the cheek.

"'Night, Mom." Lissa watched as her mother left the kitchen, then snatched Sullivan's dessert from the counter and strode into the living room.

Through the bay window, Lissa watched a flash of lightning shoot a jagged path across the sky, validating the weatherman's prediction and her mom's reminder.

There was a storm brewing, all right. And not just on the horizon. Lissa's heart ricocheted in her chest, as she set the dessert plate on the lamp table, then took her jacket from the coat rack by the door.

Even though a roll of thunder tumbled through the sky, she nixed the umbrella idea and carried the chocolate cake to the cottage. It's not as though this would take very long. She'd be out of there and back home before the rain came.

As Lissa crossed the bridge, she wished there was another way around the impending discussion. But Jared had been right. Sullivan needed to be told—and the sooner the better. No need to prolong the inevitable. Besides, he was leaving tomorrow morning, and this wasn't the kind of conversation that could be handled by telephone or e-mail, no matter how much easier it would be.

The wind whipped her hair around, and the scent of rain filled the crisp night air, promising a downpour. Lissa wanted to turn around and go home, preferring to curl up with a good book, as her mother had done. But instead of wrapping herself in warmth and comfort, living a fantasy where everyone lived happily-ever-after, she strode toward the cottage, ready to face the cold, stark truth of reality.

As she reached the steps leading to the wooden porch, she paused, taking a breath, sucking in her courage. Then she crossed the deck and knocked on the door.

Sullivan answered wearing only a pair of gray sweat pants. He didn't speak, didn't smile. And she was again reminded of a Scottish highlander, one who'd been caught off-guard and unprotected.

He just stood there staring at her as though she were a marauder.

She managed a smile. "Mom asked me to bring you some dessert."

"Thanks." He took the plate from her. "You didn't have to come out on a night like this."

"I know, but I think there's something we should talk about."

"You're probably right." He stepped aside so she could walk in, then closed the door. "Can I get you a glass of wine?"

She started to say yes, glad to have something to

hold on to, something to ease her nervousness. But wine wouldn't be good for her growing baby. "No thanks. I'll pass."

"Have a seat." He indicated the sofa, then carried the cake to the counter, where he left it.

She sat in the overstuffed easy chair, leaving him on the sofa.

The fireplace blazed, providing warmth and comfort, and her thoughts drifted to the time they'd made love in front of the hearth. She wondered whether she'd ever be able to come into the guest house again without remembering the lovemaking they'd shared, the passion. The wonder of first love. The agony of a broken heart.

"We really haven't ended things right," Sullivan said. "We could both probably use some closure."

He was right. But was there a right way to end a love affair? Lissa wasn't sure.

"We both know things are over," she said. "But it's not over for me."

He tensed. "I didn't make any promises. And with my job, I travel a lot. It's not the kind of life that's conducive to a steady relationship."

She placed her hands on her knees, felt them trembling just a tad. "I'm not asking anything from you. But I do have to tell you something."

Sullivan's stomach clenched. God, she wasn't going to tell him she loved him, was she? Or that she wanted a commitment of some kind? If he could drop his guard and make the same mistake of loving and trusting a woman again, he might take a gamble on Lissa.

But he wasn't up to the task and probably wouldn't ever be. He had too many reasons to believe things couldn't possibly work out. Still, he had to listen, hear her out. "What do you have to tell me?"

"I'm not sure how it happened, but I'm pregnant."

A roar of thunder rumbled across the sky, shaking the roof and causing the windows to shudder. But the reverberating noise didn't shake Sullivan as much as Lissa's announcement.

"You're what?"

"Pregnant. I was late with my...you know, and so I took one of those home pregnancy tests."

"There must be some mistake." He stood and walked across the room, searching for an easy way out, a hole to open up in the floor and let him escape the emotional fall-out of the bomb she'd just dropped.

"I didn't trust the results, either," she said. "So I called the doctor, and he scheduled a blood test. There was no mistake. I'm pregnant." She took a big breath, then slowly let it out. "I'm not asking or expecting anything from you. But I think it's only fair to tell you."

Fair? Hell. A part of him wished he didn't know, that she'd never told him.

But she was right. Sullivan wouldn't want a kid of his running around on earth without him knowing about it.

He raked a hand through his hair. "I don't know what to say."

"You don't have to say anything. I plan to have the baby, though, and raise him or her by myself." She tossed a strand of hair behind her, then clutched her hands in her lap. "I'm not sure how this happened. I mean, we used protection. But I guess it didn't work."

"I didn't feel confident with that first condom. It was probably expired. But I figured using it wouldn't be that risky." He raked a hand through his hair again, thinking it might be standing on end now, much like his emotions.

"Like I said, Sullivan. I don't expect anything from you."

That was good. Because marriage scared the hell out of him. And even if he wanted to lay his heart on the line again, risk betrayal and divorce, he didn't want to subject his kid to any of the things he'd been through as a child, the accusations, the lies, the guilt.

Where the hell did your mother go?

I don't know, Daddy. She went with her cousin, Tom.

She doesn't have a cousin named Tom. And don't you dare cover for her.

Thank God, Sullivan and Kristen hadn't had a child to fight over, a kid that felt responsible for a disastrous marriage, as Sullivan had felt when his folks split up. A nine-year-old boy who had testified in court, betraying both of his parents.

Wouldn't it be better if a kid didn't know his dad at all, rather than go through all of that?

That didn't mean Sullivan wouldn't step up to the plate financially. He wouldn't turn his back on Lissa and the baby.

"I'll pay child support," he offered.

"Whatever you think is fair." She looked like a windblown waif, and he felt as though he should do something, reach out, give her a hug. Something. But he stood rooted to the floor, afraid to do the wrong thing, afraid to open an emotional can of worms.

"I'll start paying before the kid is born," he added, wanting to do the honorable thing while still holding tight to his freedom, his memories, his fears.

"I really don't need anything, but I won't turn down whatever you offer." She stood. "I'd better get back inside the house before the rain hits. We can handle this over the phone and through e-mail."

He merely nodded, like a dummy on the knee of a ventriloquist, wondering if his voice would ever return.

She stopped in the doorway and nailed him with a glimmering, emerald-green gaze. "I'll love our baby enough for both of us, Sullivan."

Then she turned on her heel and left the guest house.

For a moment, he wanted to run out into the night and stop her, have her come back. Hold her in his arms and try to come up with a game plan they could both live with. But the memories of a little boy crying himself to sleep held him back.

Sullivan didn't have what it took to hold a marriage together. And he didn't know many couples who had actually been able to do so.

Lissa had lowered the boom, then let him off the hook. He could leave tomorrow and not look back.

He should feel as though he'd escaped by the skin of his teeth. But he didn't.

His emotions were wound tighter than a spring. Boy, he could sure use a stiff drink right now. Scotch straight up, if he had any available. But he didn't. So instead, he strode into the kitchen and took a chilled bottle of chardonnay from the refrigerator. He pulled the cork and poured a glass.

But somehow, he doubted an entire case of wine would soothe his nerves, still his memories and help him fall asleep.

As Lissa escaped the cottage and stepped into the night air, the wind swept a splatter of rain across her face.

The tears she'd been holding burst free, blending with the first sprinkles of the breaking storm. She'd told Sullivan she didn't want anything from him, but that wasn't true. She loved him and wanted him to love her, too. Just like the fairytales she'd read about, she wanted it all—white lace, scattered rose petals, promises and a happy-ever-after.

But that wasn't going to happen.

By the time she reached the house, the blustery wind and driving rain, along with Sullivan's rejection, had chilled her to the bone.

Shivering and trying to be quiet, she left her wet shoes on the porch, let herself inside and locked the door. Then she carried her damp jacket to the laundry room and hung it up to dry.

Never had she felt like such an outcast, so alone in the world.

As she trudged upstairs, she felt the urge to be held, to be told that everything would be all right, the way her mother had always comforted her in the past.

When Lissa reached her parents' room, she lifted her hand to knock. Paused. Then mustered what little courage she had left and rapped upon the door.

"Come in," her mom said.

Lissa entered the warmth of her mother's bedroom and found Donna sitting up in the king-sized bed, propped up with several fluffy pillows and holding a book in her hand.

"Can I talk to you?" Lissa asked.

"Sure, honey." Her mother set the open paperback down in her lap, then made room on the mattress beside her. "Sit down."

"I...uh...have a problem."

"With the vineyard? Dad's not home yet, but I'll try to help, if I can."

"No. This is a personal problem."

Donna took off her glasses, and closed the book

completely, putting it aside on the bedspread. Then she took Lissa's hand in hers. "What is it?"

"I'm…" She couldn't say it.

"In love?" her mom asked.

Lissa was going to skip the love part and jump right into the unwed-and-pregnant scenario. But love was a much better tack. And it was the truth. She caught her mother's knowing gaze, then nodded.

"Want to talk about it?"

"Not really," Lissa said, "but I think one of your hugs might help."

Her mom swept Lissa into a warm embrace, offering her love wrapped in the familiar scent of gardenia and the softness of a warm, flannel gown.

"Have you fallen in love with Sullivan?" her mother asked.

So much for keeping things a secret. "I didn't know it had been so obvious."

"Not at first, but I could sense the tension between you. It seemed far more personal than business-related. And I could also see the way you looked at each other, when you didn't think anyone was paying attention."

Mom might have seen Lissa sneaking a peek at Sullivan, but those glances couldn't have been mutual. And believing Sullivan felt anything for her would only prolong the pain, the ache.

"He doesn't love me," Lissa said.

"Your hurts were easier to deal with when you were little." Her mom gently tugged a strand of

Lissa's hair, then brushed her cheek with a kiss. "I wish there was some kind of medicine I could give to mend your broken heart, some magic words to make you feel better."

"Does that mean you won't remind me that Sullivan isn't the only fish in the sea?"

"Well, if I thought that were true, or that it would make things all better, I'd probably mention it. But I doubt you're interested in another fish right now."

"You're right. It wouldn't help. And even if I wanted to go fishing tomorrow, I can't."

"Why's that?"

Lissa took a deep breath, then slowly let it out as she prepared to bare her secret. "Because I'm pregnant."

As her mother released her arms and pulled back, Lissa braced herself for a look of shock, of disappointment, of anger.

What she saw was surprise laced with compassion. "Oh, honey. I'm sure it won't be easy to have a child without a husband, but babies are truly a blessing."

Lissa blinked. It was the second time she'd heard that very thing, words both of her mothers believed. "You're not angry with me?"

"For what? I'm not so old that I don't remember how it felt to love your father with all my heart, to offer him my love."

Lissa fell back into her mother's arms. "Thank you for understanding, Mom. I love you."

"I love you, too, sweetheart."

They listened to the sound of the automatic garage door lifting and a car ignition shutting down.

"Daddy's home," Lissa said, "safe and sound."

"Thank the Lord." Her mother froze and took Lissa's hands in hers. "Let's wait to tell him your news until after Sullivan leaves."

"Will Daddy blow his top?" Lissa asked. Her father had a bit of a temper, but usually only toward stubborn home-improvement projects and farm equipment. Never toward his wife or children.

"He won't be angry with you, but knowing your dad and how protective he is, he may want to clobber Sullivan." Mom smiled and cupped Lissa's jaw. "You've always held a special place in your daddy's heart—not that he favors you over Eileen. But you're the one who tagged along after him each day, the one who grew up to be so much like him."

All of a sudden, the adoption issue no longer seemed to matter. And Lissa began to realize she'd always been a *real* daughter. Her misconceived perceptions had thwarted her ability to accept the *real* love her mom and dad had always offered her.

"Oh, my goodness," her mother said, blue eyes sparkling and growing wide as she began counting on her fingers.

"What?"

Her mother clapped her hands and broke into a wide grin. "What a wonderful Christmas we're going to have this year! We'll have two brand-new babies to love and spoil. Two little ones who will grow up close like you and Eileen.''

How fortunate Lissa had been to be adopted by the Cartwrights. Throughout the years, their love had been unwavering. And nothing had changed. They would love her baby, just as they would love Eileen's.

Lissa's child would be blessed with the most wonderful grandparents in the world. And a loving mother. Surely that would make up for an absent father.

Now if Lissa could just figure out how to stop loving a man who didn't love her back, everything would work out fine.

Chapter Thirteen

I'm pregnant.

Those two little words had sent Sullivan's once predictable world spinning topsy-turvy.

Sleep was out of the question, and not just because of the rain pounding on the windows and the wind blowing through the trees. His mind was tossing and turning, and his nerves were on end.

A little after eleven o'clock that night, he threw off the covers and climbed from bed.

Before his marriage to Kristin, Sullivan had actually wanted a family. In his dreams, he'd envisioned two parents playing active roles in their children's lives—reading stories, playing catch in the backyard, that sort of thing.

But he'd quit believing in fairytales the day he'd come home and seen the note Kristin had taped to the bedroom door.

Dear Sullivan,
I don't want to be married anymore. By the time you read this, I'll be in Barbados…

… With someone she liked better. Someone older and richer.

After picking up the pieces that day and facing reality, Sullivan had put away any lingering thoughts of having kids.

Until Lissa made her startling announcement.

In a way, he kind of liked the idea of a little Sullivan running around, especially since his child would have Lissa as a mother. Her compassion was evident in the way she had urged her parents to bring Uncle Pete to live at the vineyard, where he could be loved and cared for by family. And her maternal streak burst forth in her love for Barney, a rascally pup who kept her hopping.

I'll love the baby enough for both of us.

And he had no doubt she would.

He figured she'd stay at the vineyard, where she'd raise their child, which is what Sullivan wanted her to do. A kid would be lucky to live here, with Ken and Donna Cartwright as doting grandparents. He imagined Donna would keep the cookie jar filled to the brim with treats.

Sullivan really liked the idea of his and Lissa's

child living at Valencia Vineyards, where the kid would grow up in peace and harmony, something that had been sorely missing from his own childhood.

It was a big relief to know his son or daughter wouldn't wake up wondering whether dawn would bring another godawful fight or a frigid cold war.

Sullivan wanted a hell of a lot more for his child than that. In fact, he didn't mind being a father and taking an active role in his child's life—after it was potty-trained of course. Little babies were scary. But preschoolers were pretty cool.

Maybe Lissa would let him take the kid on weekends and during summer vacations. After all, she was a levelheaded businesswoman, and they worked well together. Why not raise the baby as a joint venture?

Whatever you think is fair, she'd said. And sharing the kid sounded fair and right to him.

Yeah, Lissa would be easy to work with—as long as the temptation to make love didn't become a problem. And if it did? A slow smile curled his lips. They were definitely compatible physically. And their lovemaking, as good as it had been, only promised to get better with time. What would it hurt to see their physical needs met every now and then?

The more he thought about it, the more he liked the joint venture idea. It ought to work out just fine.

Unless Lissa got some fool notion about getting married and dragging a stepfather into the picture.

Sullivan's gut clenched at the thought of some other guy teaching his son or daughter how to ride a bike. Or cuddling with Lissa in front of a cozy fire, after the kid went to bed. He scrunched his face, forcing out the image. He didn't want another man to step in and take his place. But what alternative did he have, other than to marry Lissa himself?

Marry Lissa?

What kind of crazy thought was that?

She'd never mentioned anything about wanting more than he'd been willing to give. In fact, she'd given him every chance to head for the hills, to escape without having the mistake of their lovemaking haunt him for the rest of his life.

So why didn't he feel like running?

Because he liked it here at Valencia Vineyards. He liked sitting around that big oak table in the evening, enjoying a home-cooked meal, catching Lissa's eye from over the top of a yellow rose centerpiece, knowing she was thinking about the heated kisses they'd shared, the mind-spinning climax they'd just reached.

The last time they'd made love, he'd closed his eyes and let the moment and the lady carry him away. He'd opened his heart and let her slip inside.

And he'd also opened himself up for disaster, for betrayal.

What the hell had he done? Had he fallen—even a little bit—for a woman who was ready to spread her wings and fly? A woman who might move out while he was on a business trip and leave a note, explaining why the marriage no longer worked for her?

Sullivan wasn't sure, but one thing was certain. Lissa wasn't like any other woman he'd ever dated.

He'd seen that from the start.

When he'd first arrived at the vineyard, she'd been a twenty-seven-year-old virgin who loved her family and was dedicated to Valencia Vineyards. Someone who dug in her heels and lasted for the duration.

I'll love our baby enough for both of us, she'd said.

That *wasn't* the attitude of a woman who was foot-loose and fancy-free. It was the kind of commitment a loyal and honorable woman made.

Sullivan paced the living-room floor, trying to get his thoughts together.

What did he want out of life?

Once upon a time, he'd wanted the kind of home he hadn't had as a kid. He'd even tried to create a dream family with his ex. But Kristin hadn't been a dream wife.

Was Lissa a better bet?

Could Sullivan and Lissa make that old dream come true?

He peered out the window, saw the trees bend with the wind. Strong, steady. Yet pliant.

Lissa planned to raise a child without a husband. And she would let Sullivan share a part of the baby's life—as much or as little as he wanted.

But did she love him? Even a little?

She hadn't said anything about her feelings, hadn't even given him a clue that she might want a commitment of any kind. But now that he was being honest with himself, Sullivan had to admit that he'd sensed her feelings ran deep, that she'd closed her eyes, too.

Had she opened her heart? Just a crack?

The last time they'd made love, there'd been something different in the way she'd caressed him, the way she'd kissed him. They'd shared an intimacy, a yearning, a contentment he'd never experienced before.

Was that love?

If not, then why did he have this big, gaping hole in his chest when he thought about leaving the vineyard, about leaving her? And it actually ached even more to think about never holding her, kissing her or making love with her again.

He did love her.

There was no other explanation for the emotional turmoil, for the unexplainable fear he felt at losing her to someone else. And just making the admission seemed to lift a burden from his shoulders.

Now what? Did he march over to the house and bang on the door, lay his heart at her feet and hope she didn't stomp on it?

Sullivan glanced at the clock on the nightstand. 11:43—too damn late to call or go see her. But hell, now that he'd figured out a new plan of action, he couldn't wait until dawn. He needed to talk to her. Now.

He threw on a T-shirt and a pair of slacks, grabbed a jacket from the closet and slipped a pair of loafers on his bare feet.

This was crazy. Stupid. But he couldn't stop himself from going outside in the rain, from trudging across the wet grass, from banging upon the door, then ringing the bell.

No doubt about it, going out in the rain to bare his

heart and soul in the middle of the night was the dumbest thing he'd ever done. But he didn't turn around, didn't rush back to the guest house and hide—not when he'd figured out what he wanted, what he might be able to have.

In what seemed like forever, but was probably only a couple of minutes, a sleepy-eyed Ken opened the door in his robe, looked at Sullivan with a furrowed brow and grimaced.

Well, why not? It was almost midnight, and Sullivan probably looked like hell.

"Is something wrong?" Ken asked.

"I need to talk to Lissa."

Ken glanced at the grandfather clock in the entry. "It's a bit late, son. Don't you think? Can't this wait until morning?"

From the top of the stairs, Donna called out. "Ken, come on back to bed. I'll get Lissa."

But before Donna could take two steps, Lissa poked her head out the bedroom door, looking amazingly sexy and loveable with her hair hanging loose and wearing a pink-and-white flannel gown.

"Sullivan wants to speak to you, honey." Donna opened the bedroom door and gave her daughter a gentle nudge. Then she called to Ken. "Give them some privacy, Ken. You come up here with me."

Ken scratched his head and wrinkled his brow, then climbed the stairs, passing Lissa on her way down.

Lissa glanced at the grandfather clock. Just after quarter to twelve. She wasn't sure why Sullivan had come pounding on the door, why he hadn't waited until morning. After all, he'd made it clear to her that things were over between them.

He looked so…so wet and disheveled.

Was he sick? If not, he was going to be. The rain had plastered his hair to his head. And his jacket and pants were wet.

"I need to talk to you," he said, as she reached the bottom of the stairs. "And it can't wait."

She nodded, as though it all made perfect sense, but it didn't. Was this about the baby news? Or about business? She wasn't sure, but the poor guy looked like a shipwrecked sailor who'd been battered and bruised by a violent storm on the high sea.

"Do you want to sit down?" she asked, nodding toward the sofa.

"Yeah. No." He glanced down at his wet pants and shoes, then removed the muddy loafers, leaving them on the mat by the door. "Your mom would shoot me if I tracked water into her living room. I'd better stand here on the wood floor."

"Just a minute." She hurried down the hall and withdrew a spare blanket from the guest closet, then handed it to him. "You're going to catch cold."

"Thanks." He took the green-and-blue plaid blanket from her, but merely held it. Again, she imagined him a highlander—a wounded Scotsman, clutching his family tartan to his chest.

"What's on your mind?" she asked, afraid of what she might hear, afraid to hope he'd given some thought to their relationship and wasn't ready to end things yet.

"I was a little surprised at the news, so if I reacted like a jerk, I'm sorry."

"I understand."

"But that doesn't mean I don't want to be a part of the baby's life."

"Good." She was relieved to hear that much. "I can't imagine what it would've been like to grow up without having my dad in the house. He and I have always been close."

"It wasn't like that for me," Sullivan said. "My father was never around. And it seemed that both my parents had more important things on their agenda than creating a stable home for the only child they had."

"It must have been tough on you."

"More than you'll ever know." He took a deep breath, then slowly blew it out. "My dad traveled on business, and my mom got tired of waiting for him to come home and escort her to parties and social affairs. So she'd go without him. And if it wasn't a charity event or dinner party, it was a vacation with friends."

"Did your mom take you with her?" Lissa hoped so. Her child would grow up on the vineyard and have a portable crib in the office, a little baby swing, too. And maybe one of those jumpy chairs.

He smiled, yet memories seemed to cloud his gaze. "I had a nanny. Several of them, actually."

Lissa sensed Sullivan wanted to talk, that he

needed to get something off his mind, so she took his jacket and hung it on the coat rack.

"One day, my mom took me into a nearby town for lunch and a movie. We ran into a guy she introduced as her cousin, Tom. Afterward, we left her Mercedes where she'd parked, and he drove us home. But she didn't get out of his car. She sent me inside with the nanny, then they drove off." Sullivan shivered.

From the cold? Or from the recollection? She didn't know for sure, but she let him continue, hoping that sharing the memory would help.

"My dad wasn't due in from Europe for a couple of days, but he came home unexpectedly that afternoon. And when he asked where my mother was, I told him she'd gone with her cousin, Tom." Sullivan shook his head. "How the heck did I know the guy wasn't her cousin?"

"How old were you?" she asked.

"Nine or ten. I don't remember. But I'll never forget what happened."

Lissa stepped closer, took the blanket from him and wrapped it over his shoulders, hugging him without using her arms, without getting too close. "Do you want to talk about it?"

"I've only talked about it once—in court. And I never discussed it again. But maybe it's time to clear the cobwebs out of the attic."

"Maybe so."

"My dad put me in his big, black Caddy and made me point out where they'd left my mother's sporty red Mercedes. It was still in the same spot, so we waited. And waited. All the while, my dad ranted and raved, telling me things about my mother a kid shouldn't have to hear, things about her past and where he hoped she'd spend her future.''

Lissa found it difficult to keep her arms from reaching out to him, from offering comfort. She fingered the satiny edge of the blanket instead.

Sullivan blew out a ragged sigh. ''And when *Cousin* Tom brought my mom back, my dad was waiting for them.''

She was afraid to comment, to ask what happened. So she waited to hear what he wanted to share.

''My dad threw the first punch. And Tom drew the first blood. It got pretty nasty until one of the bystanders called the police.''

''I'm so sorry you had to witness that,'' she said.

''Me, too. Because I had to testify during the divorce proceedings.''

He stood there like a brokenhearted child, and she couldn't help but ease closer, offer him a hug, like the one her mother had given her earlier. And he leaned into her embrace, pulling her close. ''I'm afraid, Lissa.''

''Of what?''

''Afraid of making promises then finding out one of us won't be able to keep them.''

''Promises about the baby?'' she asked.

''No. About us.''

''Us?''

''I think,'' he said, as though choosing his words

carefully, "we ought to consider marriage for the baby's sake."

Her heart went out to him, not only for what he'd been through, but also for thinking of their baby's best interests. "Wanting to do the right thing is admirable, Sullivan. But it's not a good enough reason to get married."

"Why not? I think a sense of ethics belongs in a marriage."

"I agree. But if it's going to last, a marriage needs to be based on love."

"And what if I think I'm falling in love with you?" His voice held a soft, but ragged edge. And his tortured gaze told her the admission had cost him a lot.

She placed a hand on his cheek, felt the light bristles he'd shave off in the morning. And he gripped her wrist to hold it there.

"Do you think you could learn to love me?" he asked. "Given time, I mean."

She didn't say anything at first; she was too amazed by his words, by the evidence of his struggle. "I don't need time, Sullivan. I'm already convinced that I love you."

She loved him? For a moment, a response lodged in his throat, then the past stepped aside, allowing a new day to dawn. "Ah, Lissa. Tell me there's a chance that we can make a go of this."

She wrapped her arms around his neck and smiled. "If you love me half as much as I love you, we can make it work."

The tension and torment eased, and his heart began to swell, to mend, to flood with warmth.

"I love you, Lissa. More than I care to admit." He pulled her into his arms and kissed her, closing his eyes and letting love lead the way.

When the kiss ended, he slid her a crooked grin. "I don't suppose you'd like to go back to the guest house with me?"

"In the rain?" She touched the wet strands of his hair. "I don't think that's a good idea."

"Then maybe you'd better send me away or invite me to stay."

She blessed him with a dimpled smile. "I'm not letting you go anywhere. But if Daddy finds you in my bed, he'll probably shoot first and ask questions later."

Sullivan stiffened. "Do you think your folks will approve of this, of us?"

"Don't worry. They've always supported me in everything I've done, although I've just begun to realize that."

"So now what?" he asked. "I don't want to go back to the guest house alone."

"Then we'd better tell them. That way we can borrow some of my dad's clothes so you don't catch pneumonia."

He kissed her again, long and deep—until he thought his heart would burst. "Let's wake your parents right now."

"Mom will be excited," Lissa said. "And she'll want to start planning a wedding."

"Don't let her get too excited. I want to marry you as soon as possible, and we don't have much time to make things elaborate."

"How much time do we have?" she asked.

He kissed her brow. "My kid will probably be good at math. And I don't want him thinking I took advantage of his mom. Besides, I want to make love to you again and I'd rather not have to worry about getting shot."

"Is Saturday soon enough?"

"No, but that will give me time to reschedule my calendar and plan a great honeymoon. Any idea where you'd like to go?"

She tugged at the plaid blanket draped over him, then broke into an easy smile. "It's probably too late to pull it all together, but I'd like to walk with you on a Scottish moor."

"That can be arranged." Then he kissed her again, letting go of the past and embracing the future.

Saturday dawned bright and clear, with a spring-time promise of new life.

A small, intimate wedding would be held on the grounds of Valencia Vineyards, with only family and their closest friends in attendance.

Sullivan's Great-aunt Clara had been genuinely disappointed to miss the ceremony, but she was hosting a Bingo Marathon at the seniors' center in her hometown. And, interestingly enough, neither of Sullivan's parents could make it. His mother was on a Mediterranean cruise, and his dad had another chance to play golf at Augusta.

Lissa would have felt badly had it been her parents who couldn't attend. But Sullivan seemed a bit relieved. "It's just as well, honey. I never know whether they'll let bygones be bygones, or when they'll make a scene."

From the upstairs bedroom, Lissa stood at the window and looked over the parklike grounds, where the minister stood near a gazebo that had been decorated with lush green ivy, yellow roses and white hydrangea after being set up near the pond.

While a few guests took seats on the white chairs provided by Valley Party Rental, she saw Anthony Martinelli speak to her father, with a smiling Claire Windsor on his arm.

Lissa suspected, by the way the couple looked at each other, that there'd soon be another wedding in the valley.

A knock sounded at the door, and her sister Eileen let herself in. "The Cambrys are in the living room. Should we ask them to take a seat outside?"

"No, I'd like to talk to them first."

Eileen's gaze swept over Lissa. "You look absolutely beautiful, Lissa. I'm so happy for you."

"Thanks, Eileen. This is almost too good to be true."

"I felt the same way."

Her sister broke into a big grin, then gave Lissa a gentle hug, one that wouldn't wrinkle the dress Eileen had worn down the aisle last year, the very same dress their mother had worn more than forty years before that.

Moments later, Lissa entered the living room and found Jared talking with her mom and dad. Two teenagers stood beside him, a girl with straight brown hair and green eyes that seemed to be a Cambry trademark. The boy had hair the color of Jared's, yet seemed to favor someone else. His mother, probably.

"I'd like you to meet Chad and Shawna," Jared said.

Lissa shook their hands, welcoming them to the vineyard. "I'm so happy to meet you. And I'm glad you could come to the wedding."

"Danielle stayed home with Mark," Jared said. "Since it's a two-hour drive, she didn't feel comfortable leaving him."

"I understand," Lissa said. "After the honeymoon, Sullivan and I will come to Portland for that visit."

"We'd like that," Jared said.

There wasn't much time to chat before the ceremony, but one question pressed heavily on her mind. "Have you had any luck finding Adam?"

"Not yet," Jared said. "But we've got a lead. Something we hadn't expected. I'll let you know if it pans out."

Lissa nodded. "Sullivan and I will help with the search after we get home from our honeymoon."

"I appreciate that," Jared said.

She prayed that Jared would find Adam in time, and that her twin would be the match Mark so desperately needed.

Ken—her *real* father—took her arm. "I hate to rush you, honey, but Pastor McDonald has another wedding later this afternoon. And since he's squeezing us in as a favor to your mother, we need to get started."

"We'll talk after the ceremony," Jared said. Then he escorted Chad and Shawna outside to take their seats.

As the music began, Eileen, the matron of honor, proceeded down the grassy aisle, while Lissa held her daddy's arm.

"I love you and Mom more than you'll ever know," she told the man who'd always been there for her. The man who would be handing her over to the new man in her life. "And when Sullivan and I become parents, I hope we'll be as wise and loving as you and Mom."

A tear slipped down her father's cheek. "And I hope you'll be blessed with children as special as you and your sister."

She kissed his cheek, gave his arm a gentle squeeze, then set her sights on Sullivan who waited for her at the flower-adorned gazebo.

The sun glistened on the red highlights in his hair, again reminding her of a Scottish laird. Sullivan Grayson, her husband, her life.

In only a few short moments, they would say their vows before God and the world. Love lit his face as he waited for her to join him. And tears of happiness misted her eyes.

Sullivan couldn't believe his good fortune, as the

woman he loved made her way toward him on her father's arm.

Radiant Lissa, dressed in a cream-colored lace gown, had never looked lovelier, happier. His heart nearly burst with pride.

God had surely blessed this day, blessed their love.

Ken placed Lissa's hand in the crook of Sullivan's arm, then quickly swiped a tear from his cheek before taking his seat next to a smiling, teary-eyed Donna.

"Dearly Beloved," the minister began.

Sullivan held tightly to Lissa's hand, ready to take the journey together. Never had anything felt so right.

In response to the questions men and women had been asked for hundreds of years, Lissa and Sullivan vowed to love each other until the end of time.

And when the minister told Sullivan to kiss his bride, he did so with all the love he'd found in his heart.

Epilogue

Lissa and Sullivan had arrived in Scotland less than a week ago, and already their honeymoon had proven to be more magical than Lissa had ever dreamed.

They'd spent the first few days in Edinburgh, walking along the streets, visiting museums and art galleries, shopping and going to the theater. Then they ventured to the older part of town, where they toured Edinburgh Castle, which loomed over the city on a high hill.

This morning, they'd rented a car and driven out to Gretna Green, a village on the Scottish border where thousands of underage English couples had eloped over the years to marry legally at the age of sixteen without their parents' consent.

An anvil priest, who was usually a colorful character, would perform the marriage by asking the couple to plight their troth in front of two witnesses. And as quick as the bang of a hammer on an anvil, the marriage was legally bound.

Many an angry father had come racing after a couple, leaving the village a rich romantic history, complete with exciting and sometimes comical tales.

Lissa and Sullivan promised to return someday and renew their vows over the anvil in Gretna Green.

As the sun set on a perfect day, they checked into a local bed and breakfast, then took a walk along the cobblestone path in the lush gardens surrounding the two-hundred-year-old stone cottage.

And now, as they readied for a candlelit dinner served on the balcony of their room overlooking the gardens, Sullivan fiddled with the CD player until the sounds of Celtic music filled the air.

Lissa approached him from behind and slipped her arms around his waist. "You have a romantic streak I hadn't expected. I was the one with the Scottish fantasy, and you've done everything to make this trip special."

He turned to face her. "I never realized I had a romantic streak until I met you."

A light rap sounded at the door, and Sullivan kissed her cheek before answering. "Must be the dinner I ordered."

Instead, the elderly father of the proprietor stood sheepishly in the hall, with a teacart that held two crystal glasses and a bottle resting inside a silver ice bucket.

"Excuse me, sir," the man said, handing Sullivan a folded piece of paper. "This message came for you while you were out in the gardens."

Sullivan took the note, glanced at it momentarily, then passed it to Lissa. "It's for you, honey."

"Oh, and sir," the white-haired man said, handing him the silver ice bucket and glasses. "Here's the bubbly you requested."

"Thank you." Sullivan tipped the man, then closed the door, while Lissa opened the note.

"Bad news?" he asked, undoubtedly noticing her wrinkled brow. He made his way to her side.

"No. It's good news, actually. My mom called and left a message. She wanted me to know that Jared found Adam. They'd had his last name spelled wrong, which led them to a dead end. But now they've found him."

Sullivan sat beside her on the goose-down comforter and slipped an arm around her. "That's great."

"I know." Lissa looked at her husband, the man she would cherish for the rest of her life, and smiled. "I can't wait to meet him."

"Do you want to cut the honeymoon short?"

"Absolutely not." She socked him playfully on the shoulder. "I intend to savor every minute of it."

Sullivan brushed a kiss across her lips. "And I intend to savor every day of the rest of our lives."

Then he opened the chilled bottle of sparkling grape juice and filled two crystal goblets. He handed one to her and lifted his glass. "To a love that will last."

"Forever," Lissa added.

The crystal chimed as they toasted their love, their life and their future.

Lissa smiled over the rim of her glass, locking gazes with the man who'd filled her heart with hope and love.

A virgin's dreams and fantasies didn't get any better than this.

*   *   *   *   *

Don't miss the next Logan's Legacy *title,*
TAKE A CHANCE ON ME, by reader favorite
Karen Rose Smith, coming in March 2004!

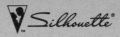

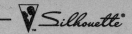

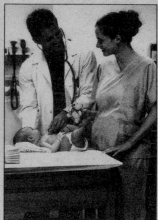

If you enjoyed what you just read,
then we've got an offer you can't resist!

Take 2 bestselling love stories FREE!

Plus get a FREE surprise gift!

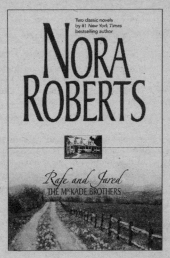
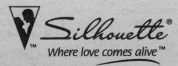

COMING NEXT MONTH